Samuel French Acting Edition

Nana Does Vegas

by Katherine DiSavino

I0589015

ıl SAMUEL FRENCH Iı

SAMUELFRENCH.COM   SAMUELFRENCH.CO.UK

FOR PRODUCTION ENQUIRIES

UNITED STATES AND CANADA
Info@SamuelFrench.com
1-866-598-8449

UNITED KINGDOM AND EUROPE
Plays@SamuelFrench.co.uk
020-7255-4302

Each title is subject to availability from Samuel French, depending
upon country of performance. Please be aware that *NANA DOES
VEGAS* may not be licensed by Samuel French in your territory.
Professional and amateur producers should contact the nearest Samuel
French office or licensing partner to verify availability.

MUSIC USE NOTE

Licensees are solely responsible for obtaining formal written permission from copyright owners to use copyrighted music in the performance of this play and are strongly cautioned to do so. If no such permission is obtained by the licensee, then the licensee must use only original music that the licensee owns and controls. Licensees are solely responsible and liable for all music clearances and shall indemnify the copyright owners of the play(s) and their licensing agent, Samuel French, against any costs, expenses, losses and liabilities arising from the use of music by licensees. Please contact the appropriate music licensing authority in your territory for the rights to any incidental music.

IMPORTANT BILLING AND CREDIT REQUIREMENTS

If you have obtained performance rights to this title, please refer to your licensing agreement for important billing and credit requirements.

NANA DOES VEGAS was originally produced by Rainbow's Comedy Playhouse in Paradise, Pennsylvania on March 16, 2019. The performance was directed by Cynthia Haynes DiSavino, David DiSavino, and Jonathan Erkert with sets and costumes by Cynthia Haynes DiSavino. The production stage manager was Rosser Lamason. The cast was as follows:

SYLVIA CHARLES . . . . Casey Allen

VERA WALTERS . . . . .Cynthia Haynes DiSavino

BRIDGET CHARLES. . . . . Rachel Faust

TOM O'GRADY . . . . .Jonathan Erkert

JOE . . . . .Jimmy Cosentino

DINO MARINO . . . . .David DiSavino

BELLBOY / CROUPIER . . . . .Joe Winters

FRANK . . . . .John DeLancey

GIA . . . . .Jessa Casner & Angela Marie Erkerk

CHARACTERS

SYLVIA CHARLES
VERA WALTERS
BRIDGET CHARLES
TOM O'GRADY
JO
DINO MARINO
BELLBOY / CROUPIER
FRANK
GIA

SETTING

Tom & Bridget's New York Apartment, and various locations in the El Tropical Casino.

TIME

Present

NOTE ON THE SET

Sylvia's Suite at the hotel is our main location, but there are a number of other locations that play an equally important part in the story.

You should feel free to be creative with how you portray these additional spaces, which include: the suite next to Sylvia's where an FBI agent tries to listen in, the casino lobby, a high-stakes roulette table, an illegal domino game and more.

In the original production, we used two turntables on the upstage left and upstage right sides of the stage that looked like a part of Sylvia's wall, but when turned, revealed the FBI surveillance suite (upstage right), and the various other locations (upstage left, which was the one turntable that kept getting re-dressed). You could just as easily do this with one turntable and a wagon, or two wagons, or even just a very specific lighting cue and a few well-placed pieces of furniture.

Crew members (dressed as gamblers, or in tuxes, or as showgirls) can move the wagons or push the turntables, or move furniture and then become part of the scenes, when appropriate.

No matter how you decide to do it, the most important thing is that each of the various locations feel specific so the audience can keep track of what's going on.

Sound cues can help when you shift to an entirely different location (for example, the first time we go to the hotel lobby or the casino floor), and using light cues to highlight the "talking room" in the moments where we ping pong between locations can also indicate to the audience where they should be looking (for example, the first time we bounce between what's happening in the FBI surveillance suite and Sylvia's suite).

Oh! And have lots of fun with the decorations. It's VEGAS, after all!

ACT I

Scene One

Sylvia's Hotel Suite at El Tropical

(This is meant to be a quick little intro scene, so you can do softer lights in this scene than you will in the true first scene that takes place in **SYLVIA***'s suite [Scene Three].)*

*(***SYLVIA CHARLES*** stands onstage, tape measure around her neck, pin cushion on her wrist, and a phone pressed to her ear. She's talking to her granddaughter,* **BRIDGET***, though we only hear* **SYLVIA***'s side of the conversation...)*

SYLVIA. *(Into phone.)* Hi Pumpkin! I can't wait for you to get here for your big bridal shower in Vegas! Remind me again what time you get in? ...OK! That's great... OK, bye! OH! Wait! Don't forget to pack an extra pair of panties. Yes. Well, you never know... Oh! And don't forget to wear those compression socks I gave you on the plane. Uh-huh. And remind me again what time you land? ...OK! OK! *I won't forget, Bridget.* I love you! Nana will see you at 5! ... 6!!! I meant 6!!! Bye, Cauliflower!

(She hangs up, takes her measuring tape off from around her neck.)

And now, Nana goes back to work!

(As she walks offstage, the lights dim on **SYLVIA**'s *suite and the flexible space [dressed as* **TOM** *and* **BRIDGET**'s *NYC apartment] rolls out on stage.)*

Scene Two

Tom and Bridget's Apartment

(Their living room, maybe. Whatever's easiest for you!)

(TOM O'GRADY [late 20s] paces on stage. He stops. Checks his watch. Paces again.)

(A car horn honks outside. TOM looks out the window. BRIDGET's cab is here.)

TOM. Bridget?

BRIDGET. *(Offstage.)* One minute!

TOM. OK, it's just, you said that ten minutes ago, and you have a flight to catch!

(TOM's phone rings [preferably it sounds something like the Pink Panther* theme song]. He looks at the screen: oh crap.)

BRIDGET. *(Offstage.)* Your phone!

TOM. Yes! Thank you!

(TOM ignores the call.)

(A beat.)

(TOM's phone rings again. Same music as before.)

(BRIDGET CHARLES [late 20s] enters, wheeling her suitcase behind her.)

BRIDGET. Man, you're popular today. Gonna get that?

(TOM quickly ignores the call again.)

TOM. You all packed? I hope so, 'cause it took you long enough.

---

* A license to produce *Nana Does Vegas* does not include a performance license for any third-party or copyrighted music. Licensees should create an original composition or use music in the public domain. For further information, please see Music Use Note on page 3.

BRIDGET. I know! Packing for a weekend in Vegas *with my Nana* was harder than I thought it would be. The outfits didn't really throw themselves together.

> (**TOM**'s *phone rings again. He pretends he can't hear it.*)

> (**BRIDGET** *stares at him.*)

Tom. Phone.

TOM. Oh! Whoops. Didn't hear it!

> (*He ignores the call. A car horn honks outside.*)

Your cab is downstairs! You all set?

BRIDGET. Who keeps calling you?

TOM. (*He hesitates.*) ...It's work. OK?

BRIDGET. Tom!

TOM. I know! I know –

BRIDGET. You've been working non-stop! How much does the NYPD need you?

TOM. Well, I AM a very valuable detective.

BRIDGET. You're the *newest* detective and everyone is taking advantage of you.

TOM. Um, if by "taking advantage of" you mean "benefiting from my work ethic and brilliant...brain stuff" then you would be right.

BRIDGET. You PROMISED you would take this weekend off –

TOM. I did say that. But –

BRIDGET. To write your wedding vows. For our wedding. That's happening in a WEEK. Because you still haven't done that.

> (*Busted.*)

> (**TOM**'s *phone rings again.*)

TOM. PHONE.

> (**TOM** *ignores the call.*)

TOM. Look! I'm switching it to silent. I'm not answering the phone. You are going to go to Vegas and have a wonderful time at the bridal shower your Nana is throwing for you. And I am going to stay in our apartment all weekend and write some vows that are totally gonna wreck you on our wedding day!

(**BRIDGET** *laughs and hugs him.*)

BRIDGET. That sounds epic.

TOM. Oh. It will be. I'll have tissues in my tux just for you.

BRIDGET. I love you.

TOM. I love you, too.

BRIDGET. No work?

TOM. No work. I promise. And you. You promise to have fun?

(**TOM**'s *phone buzzes.*)

BRIDGET. I promise.

TOM. And promise to keep Sylvia out of trouble.

BRIDGET. You mean *I* should keep out of trouble, right?

TOM. No. I mean keep your Grandma out of trouble. And Vera.

(*They kiss.*)

(**TOM**'s *phone buzzes again.*)

And text me when you land.

(*As she wheels her suitcase toward the door.*)

BRIDGET. Your pants are buzzing.

TOM. Yes. But I'm ignoring it.

BRIDGET. Mmhmm. Goodbye, Tom.

TOM. Bye Bridget! I love you!

(**BRIDGET** *leaves.*)

(*Calling after her.*) Have fun!

(*He answers his phone.*)

(Into phone.) Hi! I'm so sorry. I wasn't ignoring you, I just couldn't – no. You're right. You still want to see me today?

(He smiles, checks his watch.)

Great. Yeah. I can be there in thirty minutes. See you soon.

(He hangs up.)

(Looks around the empty apartment.)

What happens in New York while Bridget is in Vegas... doesn't need to be talked about. Or something. Right?

Scene Three

Sylvia's Hotel Suite at El Tropical Casino

(It's the living area of the suite – a lovely little seating area with a couch and a few chairs, a desk with a phone on it, and a small dining table positioned by a huge window that looks out onto the Vegas strip.)

(A door leads out onto the balcony.)

(Another door that takes you out into the hallway of the hotel.)

(And an archway takes you back to the bedroom area of the suite.)

(It's fancy verging on gaudy. So, you know, it's Vegas.)

(Three dress mannequins are center stage, each with elaborate, feather-plumed showgirl outfits on them.)

*(***SYLVIA CHARLES*** [eighties] bustles into the main room, a measuring tape around her neck, pincushion wristlet on her arm, and an enormous yellow feather boa in her hands.)*

(She's in high spirits. In fact, she's probably dancing toward the dress mannequins and sings to the tune of an old classic:)

SYLVIA.
    HER NAME WAS NANA / SHE WAS A SEAMSTRESS / WITH
    YELLOW FEATHERS FOR THIS DRESS, TO HIDE THE
    FACT THE HEM'S A MESS...*

---

* A license to produce *Nana Does Vegas* does not include a performance license for any third-party or copyrighted music. Licensees should create an original composition or use music in the public domain. For further information, please see Music Use Note on page 3.

(She trails off, fingering the hem of one of the showgirl outfits. She sighs, and begins tacking the feather boa to the dress with the pins in her pincushion.)

There we go. That's lovely!

(A beat.)

I think. It's either lovely or it's tacky.

*(The door to the suite opens, **VERA WALTERS** [eighties] enters like she owns the place. She's got a bedazzled walker, a green poker visor on, and a fanny pack that's probably filled with butterscotch candies and casino tokens.)*

(She also has a gift bag in hand.)

VERA. What's shaking baby? Is she here yet?

*(**SYLVIA** looks over, confused.)*

SYLVIA. Vera? What are you doing here?

VERA. I'm here to welcome the bride-to-be! Where is she?

SYLVIA. I could ask you the same thing. You were supposed to pick Bridget up from the airport!

VERA. Um. No.

SYLVIA. Um. YES.

VERA. Why would I do that? She's YOUR granddaughter.

SYLVIA. I'm under a deadline, Vera! The Silver Belles floor show is tonight, and I have to finish these costumes! ...You were the one to offer to pick her up!

VERA. Doesn't ring a bell.

*(**VERA** plops down on the couch, takes out her phone.)*

SYLVIA. Vera! What are you doing?

VERA. I'm texting Bridget.

(As she types.)

"Your Nana forgot about you. Frowny Face Emoji. Get a cab."

SYLVIA. Hey!

VERA. Sent!

SYLVIA. This is not how I wanted to welcome my granddaughter to Vegas. This is not how I wanted to start her bridal shower weekend!

VERA. Yeah. Someone really shoulda picked her up from the airport.

(**VERA** *is still fiddling with her cell phone.*)

SYLVIA. Vera! What is going on with you? You've been forgetful lately.

VERA. I'm eighty. I'm forgetful always.

SYLVIA. Well it's gotten *worse*. You tell me you'll meet me for lunch, and then you text me during dinner time "Where u at, boo?" You're up until all hours. You're constantly on your phone...

VERA. What are you, my mother?

SYLVIA. Thank God, no. But should I be worried? Are you stroking out on me?

VERA. I just have a hard time with my schedule! I need a secretary.

SYLVIA. A secretary? For what? To keep track of all the different buffet hours?

VERA. Nah! That's what the walker is for! People see me with that and they let me cut right to the front of the line.

SYLVIA. I knew it! I knew you don't need that darn thing.

VERA. I need it when I want people to THINK I need it! The point is, you're not the only one who is busy around here!

SYLVIA. I am running a business and costuming fifteen showgirls! What are you doing?

VERA. I...am helping you. Occasionally. I'm also a sexy widowed lady in Vegas, Sylvia! I have THINGS to do!

(**VERA**'s *phone rings.*)

(*She jumps up.*)

VERA. Gotta get this!

> (*As she crosses to* **SYLVIA**'s *bedroom.*)

It's private! I'll be in your can!

SYLVIA. VERA!

VERA. IT'S PRIVATE.

> (**VERA** *exits into the bedroom area of the suite.*)

> (*Knock, knock, knock.*)

SYLVIA. Oh dear.

> (*Knock, knock, knock.*)

I'm coming!

> (**SYLVIA** *hurries to the door of the hotel suite. Opens it.*)

> (**BRIDGET** *steps in with her suitcase. She looks...annoyed.*)

PUMPKIN SEED!

BRIDGET. You forgot me. At the airport.

> (**SYLVIA** *hugs her.*)

SYLVIA. I didn't! Vera was supposed to pick you up.

BRIDGET. Vera? Vera whose driver's license is suspended in twenty-seven states?

SYLVIA. Nevada was never on that list. Not yet, anyway. Here let me take your bags!

> (**SYLVIA** *takes* **BRIDGET**'s *purse and suitcase, stashes them in a closet / offstage / in the bedroom area, etc. Whatever works.*)

I really am sorry, Cupcake.

BRIDGET. It's OK. I'm sorry. Air travel makes me grumpy.

SYLVIA. Oh, me too. Did you wear those compression socks I sent you?

BRIDGET. (*No.*) Yes!

> (**BRIDGET** *sees the dress mannequins. Approaches tentatively.*)

Nana! Are these for the show? They're so...fluffy!

SYLVIA. Ugh. I know. It looks like a goose down comforter threw up on them, right?

BRIDGET. No! It's festive. It feels very "El Tropical."

(**SYLVIA** *is delighted. She hugs* **BRIDGET**.)

SYLVIA. Oh, it's so good to have you here! I only had to throw you a party to get you to come out here, finally...

BRIDGET.	**VERA**.
Nana!	(*Offstage.*) Who's that I hear?!

(**VERA** *enters.*)

VERA. There she is! Heya, kid!

(**BRIDGET** *and* **VERA** *hug it out.*)

BRIDGET. Hi Vera!

VERA. Sorry your Nana abandoned you at the airport.

SYLVIA. YOU WERE SUPPOSED TO GET HER.

VERA. What? Can't hear you.

SYLVIA.	**VERA**.
Stop that. You can me hear me.	What? What? I got nothing.

VERA. (*Then to* **BRIDGET**, *handing her the gift bag.*) Hey! I got you a gift. Open it!

BRIDGET. Oh! Thank you! But my shower isn't until tomorrow –

VERA. Oh, no, I didn't get you anything for your bridal shower.

SYLVIA. Are you serious?

VERA. I'll give her a buncha cash at the wedding. Sheets and towels and cutlery give me flashbacks to my first marriage. It sucked. This is a "just cuz" present! C'mon! Open up!

(**BRIDGET** *looks inside the gift bag.*)

BRIDGET. OH! WOW.

> (**SYLVIA** *peeks inside the gift bag over* **BRIDGET***'s shoulder.*)

SYLVIA. Oh wow!

VERA. Stunning right? Put it on.

SYLVIA. *(Delighted.)* Yes! Put it on, Noodle!

BRIDGET. Right now? Shouldn't I wait? For a more... auspicious occasion?

VERA. It's just us girls! Put it on!

SYLVIA & VERA. *(Chanting.)* Put it on!

> (*As they chant,* **BRIDGET** *stands and makes a show of pulling out the gifts.*)

> (*First: a visor that matches* **VERA***'s. She puts it on.*)

> (*Second: a sparkling fanny pack, again, it matches* **VERA***'s exactly.*)

> (*She does a little sexy shimmy dance as she puts it on.*)

> (**VERA** *and* **SYLVIA** *cheer.*)

VERA. Now we're twinsies!

BRIDGET. Just what I always wanted.

> (*Then.*)

Thank you, Vera. It's a really fun gift. Way better than that matching Kate Spade china set that I would use for the rest of my life.

VERA. EXACTLY. So much more –

> (**VERA***'s phone buzzes. A text.*)

> (*She ejects from the conversation and starts typing feverishly.*)

> (**BRIDGET** *looks at* **SYLVIA**, *confused.*)

> (**SYLVIA** *shakes her head.*)

SYLVIA. Vera. You're being rude.

VERA. *(Still texting.)* Huh?

BRIDGET. It's fine. I'm used to it. Tom's constantly on his phone these days.

> *(**VERA**'s phone rings.)*
>
> *(She jumps up and hustles into the other room as she answers –)*

VERA. *(Into phone, as she leaves.)* One second!

> *(**VERA** is gone.)*

SYLVIA. Really?

BRIDGET. Yeah.

SYLVIA. But he's not acting like a sketchy weirdo. Right?

BRIDGET. Honestly? He's being pretty sketchy, Nana.

SYLVIA. Oh, Cornflake.

> *(They sit on the sofa. **SYLVIA** takes **BRIDGET**'s hand.)*

BRIDGET. At first I just thought it was work. He got that promotion –

> *(**VERA** enters from the back room, but they don't notice her.)*

SYLVIA. New York City *Detective*! We're so proud of him.

> *(Sees **BRIDGET**'s face.)*

Right, sorry. Less enthusiastic about Tom. I'm with you now.

BRIDGET. He's been so...secretive. Texting, taking phone calls at all hours. Working late...

VERA. Uh-oh. Sounds like a second family to me.

BRIDGET. What?

VERA. Officer Hot Stuff is totally *Big Love*-ing you. Upside: sister wives. They make raising kids a lot easier. And if you move to Utah, you'll be so much closer to us!

BRIDGET. Tom does not have a secret second family.

VERA. Hm. You sure?

BRIDGET. *(Not so sure.)* Yes.

VERA. Let's see. Does he ever come home smelling like someone else's car?

BRIDGET. No...

VERA. You ever see a bank statement or a receipt for a fancy piece of jewelry he never gave you?

BRIDGET. No?

VERA. He ever accidentally call you someone else's name? Not his mom's name, though, that doesn't count.

BRIDGET. Ew! And no.

VERA. Yeah, OK. Not a secret second family. He probably just doesn't want to marry you.

　　　　(**SYLVIA** *smacks* **VERA.**)

SYLVIA. Or he's busy with work. Like he's been saying.

BRIDGET. That's it, right, Nana?

SYLVIA. Tom is at home, right now, writing the wedding vows he's going to read to you next week when you get married. Isn't he, Vera?

　　　　(**VERA** *is busy texting again.*)

VERA. Huh?

SYLVIA. C'mon. Let's order a bunch of room service and put it on Vera's tab.

　　　　(*As they cross to the desk area of* **SYLVIA**'s *suite...*)

　　　　(*The flexible space rolls out onto the stage, dressed as:*)

El Tropical Casino Hotel Lobby
(Check-In Desk)

(*Note:* **VERA**, **BRIDGET**, *and* **SYLVIA** *are still on stage and should pantomime their actions. They're in the background now and the attention shouldn't be on them. But the gist* *is: they're ordering food, and they can't agree on what to get. Or something like that. You decide.)*

(In the foreground, now we're in the lobby of the casino. The stage should transform – maybe a different light cue, and some casino noises [slot machines, the spin of a roulette wheel...])

*(An extra [dressed as the **HOTEL RECEPTIONIST**] is at the front desk. **JO** [forties] enters. Followed by **TOM**.)*

RECEPTIONIST. Welcome to "El Tropical" Hotel and Casino. Do you have a reservation with us?

JO. Yeah. It's under Hanks.

(Dramatically.)

Thomas Hanks.

*(Or, if **JO** is a woman, the name could be under: "Smith. Margaret Smith.")*

*(The **RECEPTIONIST** raises a discreet eyebrow, but takes the credit card **JO** offers without comment.)*

*(**TOM** waits nervously nearby with an overnight bag in hand, and enormous sunglasses on. He looks sketchy as hell. He keeps looking around.)*

TOM. *(To himself.)* Oh man. This is such a bad idea. It's cool. It's cool. Just be cool.

(He waves to someone offstage.)

I'm cool.

(Keeps pacing.)

I'm not cool. I suck. Why did I say yes to this? If Bridget finds out –

*(**JO** approaches with two key cards. She [or he] hands one to **TOM**.)*

JO. That's for you, sailor.

TOM. I'm cool!

JO. You better be cool. Nobody can find out about this.

TOM. *(A whisper.)* ...If I'm being totally honest, I'm a little nervous.

JO. Everyone's nervous their first time. C'mon. Let's get up to our room.

> (**TOM** *and* **JO** *exit, along with the flexible space.*)

> (*And just like that, we're back with the main action in:*)

Sylvia's Hotel Suite at El Tropical Casino

> (**SYLVIA** *hangs up the phone.*)

SYLVIA. Lunch is on the way!

VERA. My shrimp platter better be with it.

> (**VERA***'s phone buzzes. Text messages.*)

SYLVIA. Oh for Pete's sake, Vera! What is going on with all of these texts and calls.

VERA. How about you mind your own beeswax, huh?

> (*With meaning: a threat.*)

We're *both* entitled to our little secrets.

> (*The two older women stare each other down.*)

> (**BRIDGET** *looks between them. Lost.*)

> (*And as this mini-standoff takes place, the set expands [perhaps a portion of the wall unfolds, or another wagon comes in], and we're now simultaneously in* **SYLVIA***'s suite and...*)

The Suite Next to Sylvia's

(For clarity's sake we'll call this suite the FBI Surveillance Suite from now on.)

(You'll understand soon enough.)

(For production purposes, this "suite" can be pretty small – we don't need to see much of it. Just enough to suggest what it is to the audience.)

Sylvia's Hotel Suite at El Tropical Casino and FBI Surveillance Suite

(The door to the FBI suite opens, and **TOM** *and* **JO** *enter.)*

*(***SYLVIA*** *shakes her finger at* **VERA***.)*

SYLVIA. Vera. You promised.

BRIDGET. OK, secrets make me really nervous. Especially since the last time Nana kept a secret from me, she was almost thrown in jail. So who wants to tell me what's going on.

SYLVIA.	**VERA.**
Nothing is going on!	Your Nana is dating a mobster!

	BRIDGET.
VERA!	NANA?

TOM. I just really wish you had told me where we were going. When you said "surprise trip" –

JO. I'm sorry. Am I supposed to clear the itinerary with you beforehand?

TOM. No, it's just...

BRIDGET. You have a boyfriend? And he's...a *mobster?*

SYLVIA. He's a businessman, Bridget.

*(**JO** opens up their bag, and pulls out a windbreaker. They put it on...and it says FBI on the back.)*

*(Oh, whew! **TOM** isn't having an affair! He's working for the FBI ...and lying to **BRIDGET** about it.)*

JO. This is work, Tom. You go where the work takes you.

BRIDGET. When were you going to tell me you had a boyfriend?

SYLVIA. What are you, my mother?

TOM. I understand that. But this hotel...it's the strangest coincidence! Remember how you told me nobody could know that I was working for the FBI? *Especially* not Bridget...or her Nana?

*(**JO** begins to unpack some surveillance equipment. Maybe a stethoscope that they hold up to the wall of the suite, trying to listen to the other side.)*

JO. I do seem to remember stipulating that before I hired you.

TOM. Funny story, but, uh – Bridget's Nana lives here. At the casino. She's designing costumes for one of the floor shows.

*(**JO** stares at **TOM**. How could anyone be this stupid?)*

JO. *(Monotone.)* Wow.

TOM. Right?! It's kind of an extraordinary coincidence when you think about it.

JO. Are you pulling my leg right now, or do you really not see what's going on here, Tom?

BRIDGET. How long have you been dating?

VERA	SYLVIA.
Eight months!	A few weeks.

BRIDGET. Eight *months*?

(**TOM** *paces. Nervous. He opens his mouth a few times, but nothing comes out.*)

(**JO** *is just straight up ignoring him.*)

VERA. He runs the casino! Made Sylvie an offer she couldn't refuse. He's a goodfella, only the kind that's also part of the mob, if you know what I mean.

SYLVIA. (*To* **VERA.**) Remind me why we're friends again?

VERA. My brutal honesty and sparkling wit.

(*To* **BRIDGET.**) Dino Marino. Do the Google on him!

(**VERA**'s *phone rings.*)

Gotta take this! PRIVATE!

(**VERA** *jumps up and exits into the bedroom.*)

(**BRIDGET** *sits on the couch.*)

(**SYLVIA** *anxiously begins mixing up a drink for them.*)

(**SYLVIA** *brings the cocktail over to* **BRIDGET.**)

BRIDGET. I...feel very conflicted right now.

SYLVIA. That I have a boyfriend?

BRIDGET. Yes...and that your boyfriend is a criminal?

SYLVIA. Oh, Vera is exaggerating.

BRIDGET. So your boyfriend isn't in the mob?

SYLVIA. Well... I didn't say that.

(**BRIDGET** *gulps down her drink.*)

(*Then grabs* **SYLVIA**'s *drink.*)

TOM. OK, so I've been noodling on it. And I think I know what's going on here.

(*A beat.*)

But just in case, can you walk me through it?

JO. Oh for the love of – OK. Listen up Rookie. The Mastropietro case that we're working on? Your soon-to-be Grandma-in-law is dating someone in the crime family.

TOM. Are you telling me that Sylvia's in the mob?!

JO. ...No. I literally just told you that Sylvia is <u>dating</u> someone in the mob.

TOM. Oh. Right.

SYLVIA. He's a very kind man, Bridget.

BRIDGET. Great! So he breaks people's kneecaps with a smile on his face?

SYLVIA. Honestly, that kind of stereotyping really does a disservice to the entire Italian-American community.

TOM. So you want me to meet Sylvia's new boyfriend? Tell him to not involve my Nana-in-law in any of his illegal...thingies?

JO. What? God no. Do you want to get yourself killed? He'd peg you for a cop in two seconds and put a bullet in your head.

TOM. That sounds bad.

BRIDGET. I'm sorry. This is just a lot to process.

SYLVIA. It's not really *that* shocking is it?

BRIDGET. No, no – you're gorgeous and smart and adventurous. Honestly, I'm surprised you didn't start dating sooner.

JO. You're here to visit Sylvia. And give her this.

> (**JO** *hands* **TOM** *a jewelry box with a fancy looking tie clip in it.*)

TOM. A tie clip? Sylvia doesn't really sport neckties, Jo.

JO. It's for her boyfriend. It's got a bug built into it. So you need to *casually* give her this as a gift for her boyfriend, and ask her to invite him to your wedding.

SYLVIA. You know I loved your Grandfather very much. And this doesn't change that, Bridget.

BRIDGET. Of course I know that! Is that why you didn't say anything sooner?

TOM. But...how could I have a present for her boyfriend? She never told me she was dating somebody!

JO. You're gonna lie. And say you figured it out.

TOM. Oh man –

SYLVIA & TOM. I'm not very good at lying –

SYLVIA. – It's part of the reason I didn't say anything.

BRIDGET. *(She takes* **SYLVIA***'s hand.)* Is the fact that your boyfriend is a criminal the other reason?

JO. You've got one job, Tom.

> *(Hands him the jewelry box.)*

Go pay Grandma a visit.

TOM. Oh, yeah, I can't do that.

SYLVIA. Bridget! He's not a criminal. He just works with criminals.

BRIDGET. Oh, great. Much better.

JO. ...I wasn't being metaphorical. This is literally your ONE job.

TOM. Remember when I was all nervous downstairs and you asked me what was going on, and I was like, "I'm cool!" And you were like, "You better be cool" –

JO. Fast forward, Tom.

> *(***TOM** *hesitates. Nervous.)*

SYLVIA. Technically *I'm* a criminal, too. I haven't paid income tax in YEARS.

TOM. Bridget is here.

> *(Points to the wall separating their suite from* **SYLVIA***'s.)*

There, actually. She's visiting Sylvia this weekend.

JO. No.

TOM. Yes.

JO. You gotta be kidding me.

SYLVIA. And you *work* with criminals!

BRIDGET. No. Not criminals. Defendants. Innocent until proven guilty.

TOM. No joke. So unless – OH! I can just TELL Bridget I'm working for the FBI and I'm here on official business –

JO. NO! That would blow our cover!

SYLVIA. Well there you go! That's Dino. Innocent until proven otherwise, and I will have you know, he's as innocent as a lamb. If he weren't, don't you think he'd have been arrested by now?

TOM. Bridget wouldn't say anything.

JO. We can't risk it. If Dino finds out that the Feds are investigating, we'll be six feet under before sunrise. _Nobody_ can know you're with the FBI. Or that I'm with the FBI.

> (**VERA** _reenters. She's got a flashy sequined jacket on now, or something equally sparkly and insane._)

TOM. *(Re: his FBI jacket.)* You might wanna rethink that jacket then.

SYLVIA. I hate that damn jacket.

BRIDGET. *(Sees **VERA**.)* Whoa! My eyes.

> (**VERA** _models the jacket for them._)

VERA. Stunning, right?

TOM. If nobody can know the truth, then Bridget and her Nana can't know I'm here. I'm supposed to be in New York. Writing my wedding vows...and not working.

JO. You haven't written your vows yet? Don't you get married in a few days?

TOM. IT'S A PROCESS.

VERA. It's my good luck gamblin' get-up!

JO. You and your fiancée have ruined my entire plan, and now we have to come up with a new one.

BRIDGET. Is the plan to blind everyone around you so they can't see the cards?

VERA. I don't mess with the card tables anymore –

SYLVIA. Yeah, not since you lost half your savings.

BRIDGET. *WHAT?*

VERA. Roulette is a much more dignified game.

TOM. To be fair, if you told me what the plan was before we got on the plane, I could have warned you!

SYLVIA. We just ordered lunch, Vera. Surely the wheel can wait?

VERA. The wheel can wait, but *I* can't. Don't have much time left on the clock of life. Gotta boogie.

(**SYLVIA** *grabs* **VERA**. *Makes her sit down.*)

SYLVIA. Boogie after we eat.

JO. This is just great. You know, bringing you onto the team was my idea! And now look at you. What are you even good for?

TOM. Uh. I'm a really smart detective, Jo. I put puzzle pieces together. I'm a thinker! That's why you hired me. Right?

(**JO** *stares at him.*)

(*Knock, knock [on* **SYLVIA**'s *side of the suite...]*)

SYLVIA. Ah! See? Food's here.

TOM. Hang on. Hang on. Did you hire me away from the NYPD only because I know Sylvia? And Sylvia is dating someone who is part of the crime family the FBI is investigating?

JO. *(Yes.)* No.

TOM. Whew. Didn't think so. That'd be crazy! And kind of mean!

(**SYLVIA** *hurries toward the door.*)

(**VERA** *sighs. Checks her watch.*)

(**BRIDGET** *watches her.*)

BRIDGET. What's going on with you, Vera? You OK?

VERA. Never been better. The desert climate agrees with me. I got two great hearing aids, a bedazzled walker, and my husband finally died.

JO. We gotta come up with a new plan.

(**TOM** *and* **JO** *sit, thinking about what the new plan could be.*)

(**SYLVIA** *opens the door of the suite.*)

(**DINO MARINO** *rolls in a room service cart. Followed closely by a nervous* **BELLBOY**.)

DINO. I hear there are some ladies who lunch in here?

SYLVIA. Dino!

BRIDGET. *Dino?* THE Dino?

VERA. *(To* **BRIDGET**.*)* That's the one!

(*To* **DINO**.*)* Hey, Pin Stripes!

DINO. *(To* **VERA**.*)* Heya, Sassy.

SYLVIA. What are you doing here?

DINO. I couldn't resist!

SYLVIA. I thought we agreed that we would wait, Dino.

(**DINO** *kisses* **SYLVIA** *on the cheek.*)

DINO. Waiting is for the young. No time like the present. Besides, she already knows about me. You hear her? "THE" Dino.

(*He winks at* **BRIDGET**.*)

It is such a pleasure to meet THE Bridget.

(*He takes her hand, kisses it.*)

I've heard so much about you. Your Nana is so proud of you. And you know what I always say –

BRIDGET. *(Flustered.)* – I don't, really.

DINO. You can never have too many lawyers in the family!

BRIDGET. Oh! So you like lawyers?

DINO. I like MY lawyers!

(**DINO** *starts setting up the food at the dining table.*)

(*The* **BELLBOY** *straightens everything and makes it look better after* **DINO** *has excitedly put it down.*)

JO. OK, how about this. We wait for Bridget to leave the hotel room. You go in and talk to Sylvia then.

TOM. Can't I just give Dino a tie clip at my wedding? "Hey thanks for coming, here's a tie clip!" That's a thing. Giving guests presents. We could give EVERYONE tie clips! So it's less suspicious!

JO. It has to be today. We need the bug on him as soon as possible.

DINO. Ah! A shrimp platter! This must be for Vera.

VERA. I knew I stayed for a reason!

SYLVIA. You stayed for the shrimp?

VERA. *(Pinching **BRIDGET**'s cheek.)* And the kid!

> *(Then.)*

But mostly the shrimp.

BRIDGET. It's really nice to meet you, Mr. Marino.

DINO. Call me Dino!

> *(Buzz. Buzz.)*

> *(Ping! Ping!)*

> *(Both **DINO** and **VERA**'s phones. Incoming texts.)*

> *(**DINO** and **VERA** get absorbed, and both of them seem to be upset about whatever is in their texts.)*

TOM. Why today?

JO. There's been some talk. Someone's moving in on his territory.

TOM. Oh no. Someone else is trying to date Sylvia?

JO. No, Tom. His WORK territory. There's another crime boss in town that's cutting into his profits. Nobody knows who it is, yet, but word on the street is that Dino's boss isn't too happy about it.

> *(**BRIDGET** and **SYLVIA** exchange a look. They're both being weird.)*

SYLVIA. *(Clears her throat.)* Why don't we eat?

DINO & VERA. I'm not hungry.

(The **BELLBOY** *wheels the cart to the door, about to leave.)*

*(***VERA** *grabs* **BRIDGET***'s drink.)*

BRIDGET. Hey!

VERA. *(To the* **BELLBOY.***)* One second!

(She downs **BRIDGET***'s drink and hands it over to the* **BELLBOY,** *who is at the door [across the room from where* **SYLVIA / DINO / BRIDGET** *are].)*

(Hands him the glass.) You forgot this!

(Then, in a whisper, hands him a $50.)

Get down there and stop him from leaving.

(The **BELLBOY** *gives a conspiratorial nod to* **VERA** *and leaves.)*

*(***BRIDGET** *observes the exchange.)*

*(***DINO** *and* **SYLVIA,** *however, miss the whole thing.* **SYLVIA** *is hovering near* **DINO,** *worried about him.)*

SYLVIA. You look pale! Do you need some water?

DINO. I need some scotch.

SYLVIA. Vera, get the man a scotch.

VERA. Why me?

SYLVIA. You're already up!

*(***VERA** *looks at the door, clearly anxious to leave, but gives in to* **SYLVIA***'s demand. Pours* **DINO** *a scotch, hands it to him.)*

JO. If we can get him saying something incriminating on tape, we can use it as a pressure point. That, plus the fact that Dino's boss is furious with him – we might be able to get him to flip on the Mastropietro Family.

TOM. OK. OK, I'll think of something! Gimme a minute.

*(***TOM** *sits again. This time maybe in the classic "Thinker" pose.)*

(JO paces, frustrated.)

SYLVIA. Is it anything you can talk about?

(DINO gulps down his drink.)

(Loosens his tie.)

DINO. Corporate is – upset with me.

SYLVIA. "Corporate" Corporate?

DINO. That's the one.

BRIDGET. OK! I feel like I shouldn't be hearing this.

DINO. No, it's OK. It's – actually. Hang on.

(He pulls a roll of cash out of his pocket. Peels off a bill, hands it to BRIDGET.)

There. Now you're my lawyer.

BRIDGET. I haven't even passed the bar yet!

DINO. That's a technicality. I am employing you and your legal expertise.

VERA. Well I got none of that. I should go.

DINO. STAY.

(VERA sits.)

I'm not worried about you.

SYLVIA. What's going on, dear?

DINO. My numbers are down. We're talking beneath the concrete of an underground parking garage. And my boss – *(With meaning.)* the *big* boss. He thinks I'm skimming off the top.

SYLVIA. Are you?

BRIDGET. *(To DINO, reflexively.)* Don't answer that.

DINO. No! I just don't understand it. Our high rollers are here. They're staying in their usual rooms, ordering their usual bottles of bubbly...but they're not staying at the high-stakes tables! They keep disappearing. And my profit margins disappear with them.

SYLVIA. That doesn't make any sense.

BRIDGET. Is it possible someone else is skimming?

DINO. Somebody skims in my casino, I know about. And then I –

(**SYLVIA** *gives him a look.*)

(*Correcting.*) I give them a stern talking to!

VERA. Maybe your Whales are getting older. Saving their money up for retirement?

DINO. No. It's not that. Someone is moving in on my high rollers, and in so doing, is robbing my casino. The house don't like that. I don't like that. My boss don't like that.

BRIDGET. Nobody likes that.

DINO. And I'm gonna find out who.

VERA. Well it sounds like you have a lot going on here, so I'm just going to –

(*She dumps the plate of shrimp into the basket of her walker and leaves.*)

(**BRIDGET** *stares after* **VERA**.)

BRIDGET. That was weird. Even for Vera.

SYLVIA. She's been like that lately. I think she's upset I've been spending so much time on the costumes for the show –

DINO. Hey, the outfits look great by the way! Love this feather stuff!

(**SYLVIA** *beams, proud.* **DINO** *kisses her.*)

BRIDGET. You're not worried at all?

SYLVIA. Vera's just trying to get some attention.

BRIDGET. I don't think that's it, Nana. I'm gonna go.

(*She heads for the door.*)

SYLVIA. You're worried for nothing, Oatmeal! It's Vera being Vera.

BRIDGET. This is just too much Vera. Even for her. I'll be right back.

SYLVIA. Put $10 on red for me, darling.

DINO. Red is your color. Exquisite on you.

(They eskimo kiss.)

*(***BRIDGET*** leaves.)*

TOM. I still think that we can do my plan. We'll give him the tie clip at my wedding.

SYLVIA. Dino, be honest. How bad is this...with your boss?

*(***DINO*** hesitates.)*

JO. Dino's boss is going to have Dino killed! And if Dino is killed, our best chance of getting dirt on Mastropietro dies too.

TOM. We can't let that happen!

JO. Exactly!

TOM. Sylvia would be SO SAD.

*(***DINO*** decides not to tell her the truth – that his life might be on the line...)*

DINO. I'm getting too old for this business, Sylvia. I want to retire. Enjoy the rest of my life away from the sounds of cards being shuffled.

SYLVIA. I tried retirement once. It didn't stick.

DINO. I could be your helper. Pass you pins and hold your fabric.

SYLVIA. You wouldn't be retired then.

DINO. But I'd be with you. You're the best thing that ever happened to me, Sylvia. I just wish I found you sooner.

(They kiss. It's romantic. You can see the real love between these two people.)

You make me see what's really important. And it ain't this business.

SYLVIA. No! It's *this* business.

*(***SYLVIA*** playfully gestures to herself.)*

(They kiss again.)

JO. We have to get the leverage we need. Now. And flip Dino before he gets whacked.

TOM. And flipping him...that'll stop him from getting killed?

JO. *(No.)* Sure.

TOM. OK. I got a plan. We wait for everyone to leave the suite and then we plant the bug there.

JO. *(Genuinely surprised.)* That's simple and...it works.

> *(Buzz, buzz. Another text.)*

DINO. Sorry –

SYLVIA. I understand.

> *(He checks his phone. It's not good news.)*

DINO. I gotta go, Sylvia. I'm so sorry.

> *(He kisses her on the cheek and leaves.)*

> *(**JO** hears the door in the hallway. Runs to their door, opens it, and pokes their head out into the hall.)*

JO. Dino just left!

> *(**TOM** grabs the stethoscope and holds it up to the wall. Listening.)*

> *(**SYLVIA** sighs.)*

SYLVIA. Well I guess I'll just go...

> *(**TOM** drops the stethoscope, excitedly to **JO**.)*

TOM. I think she said she's going! This is our chance!

SYLVIA. *(Re: the mannequins.)* ...back to work. Where did I put those damn scissors?

TOM. OK. You climb on over the balcony and I'll tell you when the coast is clear.

JO. I love that plan, love where your head is at, except YOU will be the one climbing over the balcony.

TOM. Oh, no. Can't do that. I'm afraid of heights.

JO. Well, I'm your boss. So. Don't look down.

> *(**SYLVIA** exits into the bedroom.)*

(**TOM** *goes out onto the balcony of the FBI suite. Very nervously climbs [either pantomime, offstage, or however you want to do this...] over onto* **SYLVIA**'s *balcony.*)

(*He looks down.*)

TOM. (*From the balcony.*) OH SWEET HONEY HAM! That's a long way down!

(*He drops to his hands and knees.*)

(*Crawls from the balcony into* **SYLVIA**'s *suite...*)

(*And as he does so, the FBI suite [and* **JO** *along with it] disappears. Either it's rolled offstage with* **JO**, *or the wall flap closes.*)

(*Point is, now we're only in:*)

Sylvia's Hotel Suite at El Tropical Casino

(**TOM** *gets to his feet. Tries to find a good place to hide the tie clip.*)

(*Nothing feels right. He keeps moving it.*)

(*Then he hears –*)

SYLVIA. (*Offstage, singing to the tune of an old classic:*) HER NAME WAS NANA, SHE FOUND HER SCISSORS[*] –

(**SYLVIA** *enters. Carrying scissors and a bolt of fabric [we'll need this later].*)

(**TOM** *dives behind the couch to hide.*)

---

[*] A license to produce *Nana Does Vegas* does not include a performance license for any third-party or copyrighted music. Licensees should create an original composition or use music in the public domain. For further information, please see Music Use Note on page 3.

(A farce sequence ensues of **TOM** *trying to sneak out the door, and* **SYLVIA** *almost catching him. Maybe he uses the mannequins to hide and roll his way to the door. Maybe he dives behind several pieces of furniture as* **SYLVIA** *tries to figure out what that noise was. Have fun with it!)*

(At the end of the sequence, **TOM** *realizes he needs to create a distraction to get to the door safely.)*

(But the only thing he has is the tie clip box. So he throws it.)

*(***SYLVIA** *looks in the direction of the crash.)*

What on earth?

(She stands, walks toward where the jewelry box with the tie clip has landed.)

*(***TOM** *bolts for the door. Opens it. Is almost out into the hallway when –)*

*(***SYLVIA***, tie clip box in hand, turns and sees him at the door.)*

Tom?!

*(***TOM** *quickly changes his body posture so that instead of leaving the suite...it looks like he's entering the suite.)*

TOM. Surprise!?!

SYLVIA. What on earth are you doing here?

TOM. Doing here? In Vegas?

SYLVIA. Yes!

TOM. Right. Right. Right. WELL. Sylvia. I am here...to see you!

(She crosses to him.)

SYLVIA. To see *me*? Tom is everything all right?

(**TOM** *fully enters the suite, closing the door behind him.*)

TOM. Pssh. Yeah. Everything is great.

SYLVIA. So then why are you here?

TOM. Right. Yeah. Everything's BAD. I ah – I am here – because – I am – in need of...your help!

SYLVIA. My help? Doing what?

(**SYLVIA** *puts the tie clip box down on the dining room table [or wherever on your stage is the furthest away from the sofa that makes sense].*)

TOM. What a great question. Such a great question. I'm so glad you asked that very great question...

SYLVIA. Tom?

TOM. MY VOWS! I need help. Writing my vows.

SYLVIA. ...You flew to Vegas to ask for my help writing your wedding vows?

TOM. Well, when you say it like that, I guess a phone call would have done the trick.

SYLVIA. Are you kidding?! I get it! This is something you have to do face to face!

TOM. EXACTLY.

SYLVIA. Oh, Tom, this explains so much.

TOM. Thank God.

SYLVIA. Bridget was worried you were acting really strange lately, but you were just trying to keep this a secret from her!

TOM. I was? I was!

(*Then.*)

Bridget can't know I'm here!

SYLVIA. Of course not!

(**SYLVIA** *gives* **TOM** *a big hug.*)

Oh I'm just so pleased you came to ME for help! C'mon. Let's get working on those vows.

(**TOM** *sits down on the sofa.*)

TOM. (*Genuinely relieved.*) I'm so glad you caught me here because I really DO need help writing my wedding vows!

SYLVIA. What?

TOM. Nothing!

(**SYLVIA** *grabs the hotel stationary and brings it over to him. She sits next to them, and as they begin to workshop* **TOM***'s vows [in pantomime, they'll now be in the background of the below scene]...*)

(*The flexible space rolls out onto the stage, dressed as a roulette table! The high-stakes roulette table to be precise.*)

El Tropical High-Stakes Roulette Table

(*A few wealthy looking players sit at the table. A* **CROUPIER** *stands at the wheel.*)

CROUPIER. Ladies and gentlemen, a new roulette table is open right here! Place your bets!

(*These characters can be played by crew members, or maybe even a few members from the audience!*)

(*Only one of them has a speaking part:* **FRANK.**)

(*Everyone should gamble throughout the course of the scene.*)

(**VERA**, *in her super sparkly jacket, bustles in with a stack of poker chips.*)

(*She sets up next to* **FRANK**.)

FRANK. (*To* **VERA**, *quietly.*) It took you long enough to get down here.

VERA. You can't rush beauty, Frank. Besides, I sent one of my people to smooth things over.

> (**BRIDGET** *tip toes on stage. Close enough to overhear* **VERA**, *but far enough away that* **VERA** *doesn't see her.*)

> (*Maybe she's hiding behind a leafy frond of some kind. Or a slot machine. You decide.*)

FRANK. If you mean that very pushy bellboy...

VERA. *(Suggestively.)* You'll be glad he asked you to stay.

FRANK. Oh? Will I?

VERA. Well. It all depends on how much you got.

FRANK. How long are we gonna go? All night?

> (*To be clear:* **BRIDGET** *very much thinks they are talking about sex right now.*)

VERA. All night. All day. It all depends on the stamina of the people in the room. And most of my fellas know how to play around the clock.

> (**BRIDGET** *now thinks* **VERA** *is having sex with multiple people. At once. OMG. [Also, ew. Also, how?]*)

FRANK. You do come very highly recommended.

VERA. What can I say? I'm a people pleaser.

FRANK. And what currency do you take? El Tropical tokens, or –

VERA. Cash only, hot shot. But a man like you... I'm sure that won't be a problem.

> (**BRIDGET** *jumps out from her hiding place.*)

BRIDGET. Ew! Yes it will be a problem! Are you sleeping with people for money? Did you gamble your life savings away and now you're a...a...*woman of the night*!?!?

VERA. They prefer sex workers dear, it's legal in Nevada and it's their choice.

BRIDGET. VERA.

FRANK. What the hell is going on here?

VERA. Ignore her, Frank. She's getting married next week. It's addled her brain.

> (**FRANK** *nods. He gets it. He has three daughters.*)

FRANK. Weddings aren't good for people.

VERA. Also, her fiancé has a secret family.

BRIDGET. TOM DOES NOT HAVE A SECRET FAMILY.

> (**BRIDGET** *grabs* **VERA** *and pulls her away from the roulette table.*)

What are you doing?!

VERA. I can't talk about it right now!

FRANK. I'm gonna go.

VERA.	**BRIDGET.**
No, wait!	GOODBYE, FRANK.

FRANK. I know better than to upset a bride.

> (**FRANK** *collects his tokens and leaves.*)

VERA. *(Calling after him.)* I'll text you!

BRIDGET. No you won't!

> (*We're going to shift back to some action in* **SYLVIA**'s *suite now, so buckle up everyone!*)

> (*We'll play these two scenes out side-by-side, just like we did when we were in the FBI suite.*)

> (*So now we're in two places at once:*)

El Tropical High-Stakes Roulette Table and Sylvia's Hotel Suite

> (*Just remember:*)

> (– **TOM** *and* **SYLVIA** *are in* **SYLVIA**'s *suite.*)

> (– **BRIDGET** *and* **VERA** *are near the roulette table.*)

VERA. You are so bossy! You're supposed to yell at your Nana, not me.

BRIDGET. Well in a very strange twist of events, my Nana is being very well behaved, and you are SHTUPPING MEN FOR MONEY.

SYLVIA. You can't say that.

TOM. But I thought it had a playful ring to it!

SYLVIA. It's a little crass, dear.

VERA. Shtupping? What are you, a seventy year old rabbi?

SYLVIA. Why don't you try listing all the things you love the most about Bridget.

TOM. Her smile is real nice. And she's so gentle with people.

BRIDGET. I'm gonna drag you back to your room by your hair if you don't tell me what the heck is going on, Vera.

VERA. You don't scare me, kid.

TOM. She just has this lightness about her, you know? And she really *gets* people. She knows exactly what makes them tick.

BRIDGET. Oh yeah? How about I call your daughter?

VERA. *(Shocked.)* You wouldn't!

(**BRIDGET** *pulls out her phone.*)

BRIDGET. Watch me!

(**VERA** *tries to grab the phone away from* **BRIDGET**.)

(*There's a struggle for the cell phone, and* **BRIDGET** *wins by putting* **VERA** *in a choke hold.*)

TOM. She's just so nurturing!

BRIDGET. SPIT IT OUT, OLD LADY.

SYLVIA. That's good, Tom! Write that!

(**TOM** *starts scribbling excitedly.*)

VERA. OK, OK!

(**BRIDGET** *releases* **VERA** *from the choke hold.*)

(Everyone at the roulette table is watching them. **BRIDGET** *looks over, suddenly aware.)*

BRIDGET. *(To the* **PLAYERS**.*)* ...She swallowed a...shrimp. Down the wrong pipe.

(She pats **VERA** *on the back.)*

Spit it out! There we go. She's fine.

*(***BRIDGET** *and* **VERA** *walk a few steps further away from the roulette table.)*

(Angry whisper.) Talk. Now.

VERA. I'm not "shtupping" men for money.

BRIDGET. But what about all the texting? The secrecy? The – FRANK?

VERA. Frank...is a *Whale.*

BRIDGET. That's rude, Vera. He looked very trim to me.

VERA. No – he's a high roller. Lots of money. Likes to gamble...

(Then.)

With me.

BRIDGET. "With" you?

VERA. In my room.

BRIDGET. In your room?

VERA. With other Whales.

BRIDGET. With other Whales?

VERA. Why are you repeating everything I say?

BRIDGET. Because I'm hoping that when *I* say it, it'll sound less like you're SLEEPING WITH MEN FOR MONEY.

VERA. Would you get your mind out of the gutter, kid! Geez! I'm running a game.

BRIDGET. Running a "game"?

VERA. STOP THAT! Listen, your Nana was telling you the truth earlier. When Sylvie and I first moved out here last year... I got in too deep at the tables. Spent most of my savings.

BRIDGET. Oh, Vera.

(**SYLVIA** *reads over* **TOM**'s *shoulder.*)

SYLVIA. *(Touched.)* Oh, Tom!

VERA. Well you know what they say. What happens in Vegas, stays in Vegas…just turns out they're talking about your money.

SYLVIA. I'm so touched!

BRIDGET. I'm *so* upset.

VERA. No! It's OK. Because then I thought about that other thing they always say.

BRIDGET. "You have a gambling problem and shouldn't be living in a casino"?

VERA. People don't say that, Bridget. I'm talking about "The House Always Wins" – and I figured…well, I could be the house.

(**BRIDGET** *stares at* **VERA**, *realization dawning on her.*)

SYLVIA. She's gonna love it!

TOM. You think so?

BRIDGET. No.

SYLVIA. Yes!

VERA. Turns out, it's really easy to be the house! You just get a bunch of people with too much money, ply them with booze, and take a percentage!

BRIDGET. Vera, no.

VERA. And I made back my savings! And then some!

BRIDGET. From a poker game?

VERA. Nah, not poker. They got poker down here. I'm running a high-stakes dominoes game, kid.

BRIDGET. Dominoes?

(*Knock, knock. A knock on* **SYLVIA**'s *door.*)

(**TOM** *looks up, panicked.*)

TOM. Who is that? Is that Bridget?!

VERA. Everybody loves dominoes. Old people. Kids. Drunks. And it's so much fun they don't even know they're losing!

(**SYLVIA** *crosses to the door.*)

SYLVIA. Don't worry so much, Tom! Bridget has her own key. I know that knock.

BRIDGET. Vera, don't you realize what this means?

VERA. Uh, I'm a genius?

BRIDGET. YOU are the one skimming from Dino.

VERA. Nah.

(**SYLVIA** *opens the door.*)

(*It's* **DINO**!)

SYLVIA. Hi sweet cheeks. Tom, meet Dino.

(**TOM** *stands. Even more panicked.*)

TOM. DINO?

BRIDGET. You come down to HIS casino floor. You sweet talk HIS Whales. They cash out their chips, and then play DOMINOES all night in your room. You're taking his money! You're the one who's skimming! You're the one Dino is looking for!

VERA. No!

(**DINO** *is upset. And* **TOM** *doesn't make him any happier. He sizes* **TOM** *up.*)

DINO. You look like a cop. I don't like cops.

(**TOM** *backs away from* **DINO**.)

TOM. (*Full on panic.*) I'm not a cop!

BRIDGET. Dino is totally gonna whack you!

SYLVIA. Yes you are.

BRIDGET. And then Dino's boss is gonna dig you up from your unmarked grave in the desert, and _HE'S_ gonna whack you!!

VERA. I'm too young to die!

(**BRIDGET** *grabs* **VERA**'s *hand.*)

SYLVIA. *(To* **DINO.***)* He's with the NYPD.

BRIDGET. C'mon. We gotta figure out how to get you out of this!

VERA. *(To the* **CROUPIER.***)* Hey! Start the game without me tonight! I'll be there as soon as I can! And bring Frank!

BRIDGET. VERA. C'mon.

> (**BRIDGET** *yanks* **VERA** *offstage.*)
>
> (*The high-stakes roulette table wheels off stage.*)
>
> (*Now we're just in:*)

Sylvia's Hotel Suite at El Tropical Casino

TOM. I'm not a cop right now!

DINO. A cop out of his jurisdiction? *Those* cops I don't hate so much.

> (*He shakes* **TOM***'s hand.*)

But I still don't like 'em. Who are you?

SYLVIA. Dino, be nice! This is Tom.

TOM. I'm Tom!

DINO. *(Intimidating.)* Bridget's Tom?

TOM. *(Scared.)* No?

SYLVIA. Yes.

> (*Then.*)

Oh! But she can't know he's here.

TOM. I'm not here.

DINO. And why are you not here, exactly? Be specific.

TOM. Vows. Help. Vows.

> (*To* **SYLVIA.***)* Help?

SYLVIA. Why don't you go make Dino and yourself a little drink.

DINO. Scotch. Neat.

TOM. Yeah, neat!

DINO. No. Neat.

> (**TOM**, *very nervous and trying to be cool,*
> *winks at* **DINO.** *Maybe does that double finger*
> *gun move.*)

TOM. Neat!

DINO. NEAT. NO ICE. NOW.

> (**TOM** *scampers over to the bar area to make*
> *the drinks.*)

> (**SYLVIA** *crosses her arms, stares at* **DINO.**)

SYLVIA. That is my future Grandson-in-law you're yelling at.

> (**DINO** *sits on the couch, puts his head in his*
> *hands.*)

DINO. I'm sorry, it's just – things are bad. I need to talk to
you.

SYLVIA. Why? What's going on?

> (**TOM** *perks up! This could be what they need!*)

> (*He looks around for the tie clip box. Sees it*
> *on the dining room table [or, again, wherever*
> **SYLVIA** *put it that was as far away from the*
> *couch that made sense].*)

DINO. Management is sending someone. Tonight.

> (**TOM** *abandons the drink making. Picks up*
> *the tie clip box. Casually pushes it closer to*
> *them.*)

SYLVIA. …To talk to you?

DINO. I'll be lucky if they want to talk.

> (*It's still not close enough.* **TOM** *puts the box*
> *in his pocket. Hurries to the drinks.*)

I think they're here to "clean up."

> (**TOM** *dumps a bunch of liquor in both*
> *glasses.*)

SYLVIA. Clean up *you*?

> *(***DINO*** *nods.)*

> *(***TOM*** *hurries over.)*

TOM. What needs to be cleaned up? Certainly not this drink, cuz it's NEAT! HAHAHAHAHA.

> *(He hands the drink to* **DINO.***)*

DINO. What the hell is wrong with you?

> *(***TOM*** *tries to put his pocket in* **DINO***'s face. He'll do this throughout the whole following conversation. You'll know when he should stop.)*

TOM. *(So super casual.)* So...what's getting cleaned up?

DINO. I heard you ask the first time.

SYLVIA. *(Worried.)* Dino, maybe you should tell him?

> *(***DINO*** *frowns at* **SYLVIA.** *Then, to* **TOM.***)*

DINO. My numbers are down and my boss is upset.

TOM. Wow. Wow! That sounds bad. Are you scared?

> *(***DINO*** *glares at him.)*

DINO. You think I'm some kind of limp noodle?

TOM. No! No! You're a hard noodle!

DINO. What did you say to me?!

TOM. Al dente! You're al dente! You're a perfectly cooked noodle. I'm just trying to get you to talk –
(Quickly corrects himself.) To TALK TO YOU! You should ignore me. Please. Please ignore me!

SYLVIA. You can trust Tom.

DINO. I don't trust cops.

SYLVIA. He's family. And you're family. He would never do anything to hurt you, because that would hurt me.

DINO. Would it hurt you if I hurt him?

SYLVIA. Yes!

DINO. OK. Just checking. *(Firmly.)* There's nothing more to say, Sylvia.

> *(Then.)*

Except...you're changing rooms. You gotta stay with Vera in her suite for a while.

SYLVIA. What! Why? She's a terrible roommate!

> (**DINO** *is painfully aware of* **TOM***'s closeness and very distrustful. He speaks carefully.*)

DINO. Because I visit this room a lot. And if anyone was looking for me...to finish <u>cleaning</u> things, they might come here. And you might be here. And –
(To **TOM***.)* WOULD YOU GET YOUR SALAMI OUTTA MY FACE?

> (**TOM** *turns his pants-in-***DINO***'s-face into an absurd stretch to cover.*)

TOM. Sorry! I ah – I gotta stretch. Long flight.

SYLVIA. That's why you should wear compression socks. Sitting for that long isn't good for you.

DINO. Even a stuggotz like you should know about compression socks! I'll get you some. I know a guy.

TOM. Thank you?

DINO. Go stand over there.

> (**TOM** *does as he's told.*)

(To **SYLVIA***.)* You understand what I'm trying to say? It's just temporary. Until I fix this.

SYLVIA. OK.

> *(He kisses her cheek. Stands. Glares at* **TOM***.)*

> (**DINO** *opens the door to the suite.* **BRIDGET** *and* **VERA** *are on the other side.*)

> *(They scream.)*

> (**DINO** *screams.*)

> (**TOM** *and* **SYLVIA** *look at each other. Uh-oh!*)

*(**TOM** nose-dives behind a piece of furniture.)*

DINO. You scared me!

BRIDGET. *(Very nervous.)* HAHAHA, you scared US!

> *(**DINO** ushers **BRIDGET** and **VERA** into the hotel room just as **SYLVIA** covers **TOM** with a bolt of fabric.)*

Which is so silly, because you are not scary at all!

DINO. ...Right. OK. You all...have fun. And remember. Vera's room.

VERA. What? What about my room? Nothing going on there!

> *(**DINO** is gone.)*

> *(**SYLVIA** tries to act casual.)*

SYLVIA. HIIIIIIIIIII. Back so soon?!

> *(**BRIDGET** makes **VERA** sit down on the couch.)*

BRIDGET. Tell her.

VERA. No thank you.

BRIDGET. TELL. HER.

> *(**VERA** sighs.)*

VERA. OK! OK! Uh...so Sylvia? First of all, love that outfit. Don't think I told you that earlier.

BRIDGET. VERA.

> *(**TOM**, under the draped fabric, starts slowly crawling toward the door.)*

VERA. I think I might be the one that got Dino in trouble?

> *(**TOM** stops crawling. He's gotta hear this.)*

SYLVIA. What? What do you mean?

VERA. You know how somebody has been cutting into Dino's casino profits and Dino doesn't know who that somebody is?

SYLVIA. Sort of a big topic of conversation around here, Vera. Yes, I remember.

VERA. Well, funny story. Turns out that somebody is me.

  (*A beat.*)

Your hair looks so nice.

SYLVIA. How? How? HOW?

BRIDGET. Nana? Maybe you should sit down?

  (**BRIDGET** *guides* **SYLVIA** *into a chair.*)

VERA. I'm kinda sorta running a domino game from my room.

SYLVIA. Dominoes?

VERA. High-stakes dominoes. No limit!

SYLVIA. Oh my God.

VERA. I'm gonna stop though! Soon.

  (**BRIDGET** *glares at her.*)

  (*Buzz. Buzz.* **VERA**'s *phone.*)

  (**VERA** *glances at it. Looks very guilty.*)

BRIDGET. Right now, you mean. You're stopping it right now.

VERA. It's just – there's kind of sort of a game going on right now. In my room.

SYLVIA. In your room?

VERA. Yeah! There's a game going on in my room. Why is everyone repeating what I'm saying?

SYLVIA. Because we have to GO to your room! Right now! We have to leave!

BRIDGET. What? Why?

SYLVIA. Oh God. Because Dino's boss sent someone to CLEAN UP.

VERA. I mean, my room's a little messy, but –

SYLVIA. No!

  (*Mimes shooting.*)

CLEAN. UP. And they might come here! And clean US up!

(**TOM** *stands bolt upright, totally freaked!*)

(*Bang, bang, bang. Heavy knocks on the door.*)

(*He stumbles backwards into the light switch on the wall.*)

(*The room plunges into darkness.*)

(**SYLVIA** *jumps up, shoos* **TOM** *away from the light switch.*)

BRIDGET. What just happened?

SYLVIA. (*A whisper.*) Uhhhh… I turned off the lights!

(*He drops back down to the floor. Acts like an ottoman.*)

BRIDGET. WHY?

(*Bang, bang, bang! More knocks!*)

VERA. Is that –?

BRIDGET. "Housekeeping"?

VERA. What do we do?!

SYLVIA. Just keep quiet! They'll go away.

(*Beep!*)

(*A keycard in the lock.*)

(*The door swings open. And if you can do it, the hallway should be super bright. So we can't quite see who is in the door.*)

(*But their long shadow should fall into the room.*)

(*And man this person seems scary! This is totally the guy* **DINO**'*s boss sent to whack them!!!!!*)

VERA. TAKE THE LITTLE ONE FIRST!

ACT II

Scene One

Sylvia's Hotel Suite at El Tropical and FBI Surveillance Suite

(A long shadow looms in the doorway.)

(BRIDGET, SYLVIA, VERA *[and a hidden-beneath-some-fabric* **TOM***] all cower in the darkened hotel suite.)*

(Basically it's the same as the Act I ending, except that the adjoining FBI suite is now visible.)

(JO *is listening at the wall to* **SYLVIA***'s suite with the stethoscope.)*

VERA. DON'T SHOOT!!!!

(The lights in **SYLVIA***'s suite turn on, revealing* **GIA MASTROPIETRO** *[twenties] in the doorway. Hand on the light switch.)*

(She's dressed like a modern, edgy business woman. Think Emily Blunt in The Devil Wears Prada. *Chic and tough. Maybe a little too much eyeliner, and maybe she teased her hair a little too much. But, like, if you told her that, she would probably punch you in the face.)*

(**GIA** *may seem nice here, but let's be real: she is a bad guy, and she's terrifying beneath the bubbly act.*)

SYLVIA. *(Wary.)* Who are you?

GIA. *(Intense, angry.)* Are you Sylvia?

SYLVIA. I really want to say no, and I don't know why.

(**GIA** *screams excitedly, runs at* **SYLVIA.**)

GIA. AUNT SYLVIA!

(*She wraps her arms around* **SYLVIA** *and hugs her tightly.* **SYLVIA**'s *arms are pinned to her sides.*)

SYLVIA. She's so tiny! But I'm still scared!

VERA. First Tom has a secret family, and now you have a secret niece? Why am I always the last to know?

BRIDGET. *(To* **GIA.**) Hi – um, who are you and why are you hugging my Nana and how did you get into our suite?

(**GIA** *turns to look at* **BRIDGET.** *All warmth completely gone.*)

(*She lets go of* **SYLVIA.**)

(**BRIDGET** *takes a few steps back, very intimidated.*)

(*A beat. Then.*)

GIA. *(Happy.)* YOU MUST BE BRIDGET!

(**GIA** *grabs* **BRIDGET** *and hugs her tight.* **BRIDGET**, *wide-eyed, looks at* **SYLVIA.**)

BRIDGET. *(A whisper to* **VERA** *as* **GIA** *hugs her.)* What is happening?

VERA. I never know what's happening.

GIA. *(Still hugging* **BRIDGET.**) Oh my gosh, I've just been dying to meet you both!

BRIDGET. *(Still being hugged.)* Yaaaaay. Whyyyyyy?

(**GIA** *finally releases* **BRIDGET.**)

GIA. Oh. My. Gawd. My manners! I'm Gia. Sylvia is dating my Uncle Dino.

(**JO** *gasps from the FBI suite.*)

JO. GIA?! As in GIA Mastropietro? Did she –?

(*Looks around the empty room.*)

Ugh. You're no help.

BRIDGET. Oh! So you're *related* to Dino?

GIA. No.

(*Suddenly intense.*)

But he IS family.

VERA. How can he be family if you're not related?

(*It dawns on her.*)

OH.

SYLVIA. (*Wide-eyed.*) Oooooh. Oh! Oh. OK! How nice to meet you.

GIA. Sorry I just let myself in here. I got a master key.

(*She holds up the key card, all bubbly again.*)

My Grandpa owns this casino. I was just so excited to finally meet you.

(*Then, intense, to* **BRIDGET.***)* You got a problem with that?

BRIDGET. Nope. No problems here that I would want to talk about.

(**JO** *straightens up.*)

(*Opens up a briefcase. Pulls out a laptop.*)

JO. He better have planted that bug or died trying.

(**JO** *puts headphones in. Listens.*)

VERA. So... Dino works for your Grandfather?

GIA. (*With a smile.*) For now.

(*Then.*)

I'm actually looking for him. Have you seen him?

VERA. Your Grandpa? Never met him.

GIA. No. Dino.

JO. *(Rips the headphones off.)* Ugh. It's all muffled! It's like the bug is under a blanket or something.

> *(**TOM** starts crawling toward the door, underneath his bolt of fabric.)*

> *(**GIA** counters on the other side of the stage. She's gonna spot **TOM**.)*

> *(**SYLVIA** kicks **TOM** to stop him from moving, then hurries over to **GIA** and gently guides her away from where **TOM** is.)*

SYLVIA. Well it is so nice to meet you, dear.

> *(**GIA** inspects the costumes on the mannequins.)*

GIA. *(Genuinely surprised.)* Hey, these are nice. You make these?

SYLVIA. Sure did!

GIA. Doesn't the Silver Belles show open tonight? I see some unfinished hems, here.

BRIDGET. Boy. You are observant.

> *(**JO** goes back to listening at the suite wall with the stethoscope.)*

GIA. Well. I'm gonna be running this casino one day soon.

VERA. Doesn't Dino run this casino?

> *(**GIA** smiles at her.)*

GIA. Mmhmm. For now. But he's gonna be retired.

> *(**BRIDGET** and **VERA** share a scared look.)*

> *(**TOM** squeaks in surprise and fear. **SYLVIA** mimics the noise to cover.)*

SYLVIA. He's – what?

GIA. *(Loudly.)* RETIRE. He's going to RE-TIRE.

> *(Then.)*

Anyway, my Grandfather has been training me to take over for Dino these past couple of months. Ever since Dino's mind started to wander away from the business.

(She rubs SYLVIA's back.)

And who can blame him, huh? You're very distracting.

(Then.)

So has he told you anything about…you know. Business stuff? Here. At the casino?

BRIDGET. NOPE!

SYLVIA. We don't talk.

(Correcting.)

About business! We don't talk about business. Never mix work and pleasure!

*(**GIA** smiles coldly and then turns to **BRIDGET**.)*

GIA. What about you?

VERA. Bridget's never experienced pleasure. Too high strung.

BRIDGET. Thanks a lot.

VERA. Tell me I'm lying!

GIA. *(To **BRIDGET**.)* You and that fiancé of yours…you ever talk about _his_ work?

BRIDGET. You know about Tom?! How? Wow! …How?

VERA. Oh my God, are you Tom's secret wife?

*(**GIA** laughs. It is terrifying.)*

GIA. I would never marry a Fed!

*(**VERA** and **BRIDGET** stare at **GIA**, confused.)*

*(And while they look at **GIA**, **TOM** pops up from under his bolt of fabric – his cover literally and metaphorically blown. **SYLVIA** stares at him.)*

SYLVIA. *(Looking at **TOM**.)* A FED?

*(**VERA** is extremely amused by this. She laughs.)*

VERA. Sure. Tom's with the FBI and I've only been married twice.

BRIDGET. He's with the NYPD.

GIA. No, he's not.

(**SYLVIA** *stares at* **TOM**. *Is this true?*)

(**TOM** *nods. Yup.*)

BRIDGET. Yes. He is.

GIA. (*Sweet as pie.*) Two things you should know about me, *Bridget.* I make it a point to know everything that's going on in my casino, and with my family.

VERA. What's the second thing?

GIA. Being told I'm wrong – especially when I'm not – makes me very angry.

(**TOM** *pantomimes to* **SYLVIA**, *pointing at the door. He's asking her to help him get out of there.*)

VERA. We don't want that! Don't be angry!

JO.	GIA.
Don't make her angry!	Don't make me angry.

(*The realization that* **TOM** *has been lying to her hits* **BRIDGET**.)

(*She sits down on the sofa, confused.*)

BRIDGET. But – but…he never told me that. How can that be true?

(**TOM** *starts crawling toward the balcony door.* **SYLVIA** *uses her body to shield him.*)

VERA. Oh! Oh! It wasn't a secret family after all! It was a secret job! You hearing this, Sylvie?

(**VERA** *turns to look at* **SYLVIA**.)

(**SYLVIA** *grabs the fabric off of* **TOM** *and holds it up like a curtain in front of her [and* **TOM***], hiding him from their view.*)

SYLVIA. WOW. Yeah. Uh-huh.

GIA. *(To* **SYLVIA**, *suspiciously.)* What are you doing?

SYLVIA. I am measuring this fabric. To finish those costumes up.

GIA. Where's your measuring tape?

SYLVIA. ...I'm self-taught. I do not measure with tape. I measure with wing span.

> (**BRIDGET** *covers her face with her hands.)*

BRIDGET. I'm an idiot.

> (**GIA**'s *attention goes back to* **BRIDGET**. *And as soon as it does,* **SYLVIA** *opens the balcony door and boots an already-crawling-out-the-door* **TOM** *out of the door.)*

GIA. As a woman, I'm very upset on your behalf that he didn't tell you he took a job with the FBI.

> *(Then, with meaning.)*

As a *business* woman...it's good for you that he didn't.

> (**TOM** *shimmies across the balcony, back into the FBI suite.)*

> (**VERA**'s *phone starts ringing. She ignores it.)*

Knowing too much is a dangerous thing.

BRIDGET. Ominous yet comforting, Gia.

> (**GIA** *pats her back.)*

> (**VERA**'s *phone rings again.)*

JO. *(To* **TOM**.) What are you doing?

TOM. Escaping my death!

GIA. I tend to have that affect on people.

> *(Re:* **VERA**'s *phone.)*

Are you gonna get that or what?

> (**VERA** *feigns surprise.)*

VERA. Oh! I didn't even hear it –

> *(Points to her ears.)*

Hearing aids! Can't live with 'em, can't replace the batteries once they die. Arthritis.

(**VERA** *silences the phone call.*)

JO. Death by mobster?

TOM. Death by Bridget! I am glad that's over, because I'm not going back in there.

(**JO** *points to the box-shaped lump in* **TOM**'s *pocket [where he has put the tie clip box].*)

JO. Well, unless you're just happy to see me – you're gonna have to go back and plant that bug.

GIA. So. Sylvia. About business –

SYLVIA. The costumes will be finished! Just have to find my scissors.

(**SYLVIA** *searches for her scissors.*)

JO. And forget about leaving the bug in the room. You gotta plant it on Gia.

TOM. She's not wearing a tie. Also... NO.

GIA. It's not about the costumes.

JO. Just clip it on her somewhere. If we can get ears on Gia Mastropietro, we might just be able to blow this whole case wide open! Especially if she's wired up when she kills Dino!

(**GIA** *finds the scissors and holds them up. Is she gonna throw them at* **SYLVIA***?!!?*)

(*No, that's silly. She wouldn't do that. Not with so many witnesses around.*)

(**GIA** *hands the scissors to* **SYLVIA**.)

TOM.	**GIA**.
...She's gonna *kill* Dino?	I gotta to talk to Dino.

JO. Would you keep up, Thomas?!

(**SYLVIA**'s *eyes go wide. She and* **BRIDGET** *and* **VERA** *all exchange a look. This can't be good.*)

GIA. It's time sensitive.

SYLVIA. Oh? Can I give him a message for you?

JO. Go! Clip!

> (**TOM** *takes a big breath and heads back out onto the balcony.*)
>
> (*He shimmies over to* **SYLVIA***'s balcony, and watches from the window – nobody is looking!*)
>
> (*He opens the door, and takes cover underneath the dining room table.*)

GIA. Nah. This kind of business needs to be "discussed" in person.

SYLVIA. Face to face?

GIA. It's harder when they're looking at you, but sure.

VERA. OK, well, he's not here! So you should go.

GIA. But we're just getting to know each other! Just a couple of gals. Palling around.

VERA. Well, then, I should go!

> (**VERA** *stands, phone in hand.*)
>
> (**BRIDGET** *stares at her.*)

BRIDGET. No. You shouldn't!

> (*As* **VERA** *walks to the door, her phone buzzes again –*)

VERA. Yes. I need to.

GIA. *(Suspicious.)* Everything OK?

BRIDGET.	**VERA.**
(To **VERA.***)* NO.	*(To* **GIA.***)* Yes!

> (**BRIDGET** *casts a panicked look to* **SYLVIA***. Help.*)

SYLVIA. Ah! Gia! Can you help me? Hold this while I pin it!

> (**SYLVIA** *pulls* **GIA** *over to the mannequins [***GIA** *should be standing on the side closest to the table, where* **TOM** *is hiding].*)

    (**SYLVIA** *and* **GIA**, *their backs to the audience, work on the dress mannequin.*)

VERA. *(A whisper, to* **BRIDGET**, *waving her phone at her.*) I gotta bunch of angry Whales in my room. I gotta go!

    (**TOM** *crawls out from under the table, he opens the tie clip box and takes out the tie clip. Holds it up!*)

BRIDGET. *(A whisper.)* You said you had taken care of that!

    (**TOM** *crawls toward* **GIA**, *whose back is to him.*)

VERA. *(A whisper.)* I got distracted! Listen, I'll go take care of it now.

    (**TOM** *tries to clip the tie clip bug on* **GIA**.)

    (*Fails.*)

BRIDGET. *(A whisper.)* You better.

    (**SYLVIA** *sees* **TOM**.)

    (**TOM** *freezes in panic.*)

    (**SYLVIA** *freezes in panic.*)

    (**GIA** *looks at* **SYLVIA**.)

GIA. Sylvia? What are you – [looking at]?

    (*As* **GIA** *turns to see what* **SYLVIA** *is staring at [which is* **TOM***],* **SYLVIA** *grabs* **GIA** *and hugs her, tight.*)

SYLVIA. Thank you so much for helping meeeee! You're so nice!

    (**SYLVIA** *holds* **GIA** *in place so she can't turn her head. And this time, it's* **GIA**'s *arms who are pinned to her sides.*)

    (**TOM** *quickly clips the tie clip to* **GIA** *somewhere [it'll depend on how you costume her, but the gist is: bottom of suit jacket, bottom of skirt hem, bottom of pant leg, etc.].*)

(**TOM** *waves apologetically at* **SYLVIA** *and books it out onto the balcony.*)

(*As* **VERA** *leaves out the front door of the suite –*)

BRIDGET. (*A shouted whisper.*) And no game!

(**GIA** *and* **SYLVIA** *stare at* **BRIDGET.**)

(**BRIDGET** *turns to face them:*)

...She has a gambling problem. A BIG one.

(**GIA** *narrows her eyes at* **BRIDGET.** *She's not buying this.*)

(**BRIDGET**, *however, doesn't notice. Because over* **GIA**'*s shoulder, she sees* **TOM** *on the balcony.*)

(*Her jaw drops open.*)

(**TOM** *and* **BRIDGET** *stare at each other. Remember, only* **SYLVIA** *and* **DINO** *know* **TOM** *is in Las Vegas until this moment.*)

(*So, uh-oh!*)

(*Utterly flabbergasted.*)

Wha – wha – wha –?

(**TOM** *starts shimmying to the safety of the FBI suite.*)

SYLVIA. (*Covering.*) Water? You got it!

(**SYLVIA** *hurries to get a glass of water.*)

(**GIA** *turns to look at the balcony where* **BRIDGET** *is staring...but* **TOM** *is gone.*)

(*He's back in the FBI Suite.*)

JO. Done?

TOM. Done for. Bridget is gonna kill me.

(**JO** *grabs the laptop, puts the headphones in.*)

BRIDGET. I'm gonna kill him.

JO. Hey, at least you did one thing right. The bug is working.

> (**JO** *unplugs the headphones and turns the volume up on the computer.* **JO** *and* **TOM** *can now hear what's going on in the other room.*)

> (**BRIDGET** *ignores* **GIA.** *She goes to the balcony, opens the door, sticks her head out. But* **TOM***'s not there.*)

GIA. Who is she killing?

SYLVIA. Pigeons. She hates birds. Male birds.

BRIDGET. Male birds who LIE.

> (**SYLVIA** *grabs* **BRIDGET,** *puts an arm around her.*)

GIA. Mmhmm. And that friend of yours – where did she go?

BRIDGET. *(Straining to look out the window, distracted.)* Her room.

> (**SYLVIA** *elbows her.*)

Owwwwooohhh. Right. The casino. She went down to the casino. To...uh...

SYLVIA. *(C'mon* **BRIDGET.***) Gamble.*

GIA. Mmhmm. And she wouldn't be going to meet with some of the casino's most prominent high rollers and engage them in an illegal game that she's running on the casino premises?

> (**TOM** *and* **JO** *look at each other.*)

> (**SYLVIA** *and* **BRIDGET** *look at each other.*)

BRIDGET.   **SYLVIA.**
Whaaaaaaaat?   Of course not!

BRIDGET. That's just...that'd be totally INSANE to do something like that. She wouldn't –

SYLVIA. – Never in a million years.

JO. *(To* **TOM.***)* Would she?

TOM. *(Without hesitation.)* Yes.

> *(***JO*** *takes off their FBI wind breaker. And their pants.)*

(Re: the undressing.) Whoa! Whoa! Whoa!

> *(Averting his eyes.)*

A little warning before you do that, please!

JO. I'm going undercover!

TOM. It doesn't look like it!

SYLVIA. *(As bravely and firmly as she can.)* I'm not really sure what you're trying to imply, here, Gia. But I'm suddenly getting the distinct impression that you are not here to "pal around with the gals."

> *(***JO*** *puts on a pair of nice pants and a blazer.)*

> *(***JO*** *puts on a pair of fake glasses and some jewelry. They look pretty fancy now. Or ridiculous. Your choice.)*

JO. We gotta act fast otherwise our whole plan is gonna go up in smoke. But don't worry, Rookie. I have an idea.

> *(***JO*** *leaves.)*

> *(***TOM*** *stares after* ***JO.***)*

TOM. Nothing good ever happened from someone saying that.

> *(He turns his attention back to the laptop. Listening. And maybe chewing anxiously on his fingernails.)*

> *(***GIA*** *advances toward* ***SYLVIA*** *and* ***BRIDGET.** She is no longer trying to be warm and friendly.)*

GIA. A lot of people underestimate me. And it's their last mistake.

> *(***GIA*** *heads towards the door.)*

If you see your friend before I do, tell her I'd like a word. Privately. Same goes for Dino.

(**GIA** *opens the door. Then, to* **BRIDGET**.)

Oh, and same for that fiancé of yours. I hear he's in town, too.

(**GIA** *leaves.*)

(**TOM** *freaks out.*)

(**SYLVIA** *and* **BRIDGET** *freak out.*)

(*After a minute –*)

BRIDGET. What do we do?! What do we do?!

SYLVIA. We need a plan!

BRIDGET. What's the plan?

SYLVIA. OK. OK. Step one. Everybody avoids Gia. We gotta text Vera and Dino. They have to dodge that teeny tiny mobster like the plague.

(**TOM** *is still freaking out. He tries hiding in his room.*)

BRIDGET. OK. What's step two?

SYLVIA. I have to finish these costumes.

BRIDGET. The – the costumes?

SYLVIA. The show must go on, Bridget.

BRIDGET. OK. OK. Step three. I'm gonna go kill Tom.

SYLVIA. You can't kill Tom, that creates too many additional steps, Pumpkin! Step four, get the body out of the hotel, step five, drive the body to the desert, step six, dig a _hole_ –

BRIDGET. FINE. But I'm gonna go yell at him at least.

SYLVIA. After you yell at him, bring him back here, because he can't run into that mini-Mafiosa either.

BRIDGET. OK. Step three, yell at Tom.

SYLVIA. Step four, everybody meets back here. And then we'll figure out step five.

(Before **SYLVIA** *can stop her,* **BRIDGET** *exits the suite the same way* **TOM** *did – over the balcony!)*

Bridget! Not the balcony!

(As she watches her climb across the window.)

Oh dear. Kids these days.

*(***SYLVIA*** *turns to look at the dress mannequins. She gets an idea.)*

...Hello step five!

(She wheels the mannequins offstage, into her bedroom.)

(The lights go out on **SYLVIA***'s empty suite [but remain up on the FBI suite].)*

(The flexible space rolls out, center stage, dressed as:)

Vera's Illegal Domino Game (In Her Hotel Room) and the FBI Surveillance Suite

(A raucous high-stakes dominoes game is being played.)

*(***VERA*** *is the keeper of the "Boneyard" [AKA: the dealer].)*

*(***FRANK*** *is there! And a bunch of other high rollers.)*

VERA. This is the last round, everyone! We gotta cut the game short tonight.

(Everyone boos **VERA***.)*

Pipe down or I take the pot for myself and we end this now!

(They quiet down.)

That's more like it. OK! Last bets in!

(Chatter as everyone places their bets.)

*(There's a knock at both doors [**VERA**'s and **TOM**'s].)*

*(**VERA** hurries over, opens it and **JO** [in their fancy outfit] steps inside.)*

JO. *(Doing what they think is a "fancy" accent.)* Hullo! I'm here for the game, daaaahling.

> *(**VERA** sizes **JO** up as the room behind her grows quiet.)*

> *(**TOM** hurries to open his door.)*

> *(**BRIDGET** storms in.)*

BRIDGET. HELLO?

VERA. What's the password?

TOM. Uh – um – surprise!

JO. Uh – the password? The password is money, daaaahling.

> *(**JO** holds up a roll of bills.)*

VERA. There is no password, but if there were, that would be it.

BRIDGET. What's the surprise?! You being in Las Vegas? You being in Las Vegas FOR WORK when you promised me you would take time off to write your wedding vows? Or the BIGGEST SURPRISE, which is, hey, you don't work for the NYPD! You work for the FBI! Which, normally, I would find totally sexy!

TOM. Yeah? Sexy is good!

BRIDGET. I DON'T FIND IT SEXY RIGHT NOW.

JO. So can I come in?

VERA. No. You can scram. There's no gambling here. Just a couple of friends having fun.
(To the room.) Isn't that right?

> *(The gamblers enthusiastically agree with **VERA**.)*

*(**VERA** turns back to **JO**, arms crossed over her chest.)*

TOM. For the record, I actually did a bunch of work on my wedding vows and they're basically done!

BRIDGET. Congratulations? Do you want me to throw you a ticker tape parade? You've been LYING TO ME for MONTHS.

*(**JO** pulls **VERA** to the side.)*

JO. OK, fine. I'm not really here to join your game. I'm here to warn you! You're in danger. But I can help you.

(Conspiratorially.)

I'm with the FBI. And if you're willing to cooperate, I can protect you.

*(**VERA** sizes **JO** up.)*

*(Behind her, **FRANK** swaps out one of his tiles, thinking no one is watching.)*

TOM. Bridget, I'm so sorry.

BRIDGET. Not as sorry as you're gonna be when *The Goddaughter* puts your feet in cement and drops you off the Hoover Dam!

VERA. "Cooperate," huh? Listen. I'm eighty years old. I've had three husbands, and each one of you would tell you the same thing.

JO. Let me guess. You don't cooperate?

VERA. No. Vera Walters is no snitch. Now get the hell out of my room!

*(**VERA** pushes **JO** out of the room. Slams the door.)*

(Turns back to the players.)

Frank, I saw you swap a tile out. This ain't my first rodeo. Pull that crap again, you'll never set foot in another one of my games. Got it?

FRANK. *(Humbled.)* Yeah. Sorry, Vera.

GIA'S VOICE. *(Through* **TOM***'s computer.)* Ciao!

> (**BRIDGET** *tackles* **TOM** *to the ground.)*

BRIDGET. Get down! It's Gia!

> (**TOM** *pops up, points to the computer.)*

TOM. It's OK! It's coming from my laptop! I planted a bug on her!

> *(Then.)*

But if it had really been Gia, you just tried to save me.

BRIDGET. Well, yeah. I love you.

VERA. Let's re-shuffle. Last hand, everybody ante up –

> *(The door to the suite bangs open.)*

> (**DINO** *stands in the doorway.)*

Everybody out! Out, out, out!

> *(All the high rollers scurry out of the suite.)*

> (**VERA** *tries to follow them out, but* **DINO** *stops her.)*

DINO. VERA.

GIA'S VOICE. *(Through* **TOM***'s computer.)* How are you, Nonno?

TOM. Oh! Oh! She's talking to her Grandpa! He's the head of the –

BRIDGET. Yeah, yeah. I already got the recap.

> *(They huddle in front of the computer, listening.)*

VERA. I am shocked! Shocked to find gambling is going on in here!

DINO. Don't you quote *Casablanca* to me!

> (**VERA** *takes a big breath, closes her eyes.)*

VERA. Fine. You got me. If you're gonna whack me, do it quick.

DINO. I admit I was not pleased when I discovered YOU are the reason my numbers are down, and my boss wants to have me retired. Permanently...

VERA. I didn't know I was causing so much trouble, Dino! I needed money, and you don't have any domino tables downstairs. And everybody loves dominoes!

DINO. I know! Hell, *I* love dominoes! Why didn't I think of adding this to the games?

GIA'S VOICE. *(Through* **TOM***'s computer.)* I went to the thief's hotel room –

BRIDGET. Vera!

GIA'S VOICE. *(Through* **TOM***'s computer.)* But I saw one of the FBI agents go inside.

TOM. Jo!

GIA'S VOICE. *(Through* **TOM***'s computer.)* I'm back on the casino floor. Can't make a move yet.

VERA. Wait, so are you mad?

DINO. Oh, I'm furious. But I'm also impressed! And if we can get out of this mess – that, to be clear, you created – I got a business offer for you.

GIA'S VOICE. *(Through* **TOM***'s computer.)* No, the granddaughter and the girlfriend don't seem to be directly involved, but I think the safest way is to take care of them all.

VERA. So it's a "no" to the whacking me?

DINO. No whacking. Just working! Work with me, Vera! Co-managers. It'll give me more time to spend with that beautiful broad on the fourteenth floor.

VERA. Wow, that sounds so romantic... You ARE talking about Sylvia, right?

DINO. Yeah. But we gotta figure a way out of this. Sylvia texted. Let's get up to her room.

VERA. OK. If you see a tiny ball of feminine fury, RUN.

GIA'S VOICE. *(Through* **TOM***'s computer.)* I knew you would agree. None of them will be a problem for you any longer.

DINO. *(With a shiver.)* Gia. So small. So terrifying.

  *(**DINO** and **VERA** exit.)*

  (The flexible space disappears / rolls offstage.)

  (Now we're just in:)

FBI Surveillance Suite

GIA'S VOICE. *(Through **TOM**'s computer.)* I love you! Give Grandma a big hug for me!

  *(**TOM** and **BRIDGET** look at each other.)*

  *(Oh. Crap. They freak out – but then **TOM** pauses:)*

TOM. Hold on! Hold on! When she says, "Take care of them all –" she IS talking about killing us, right?

BRIDGET. YES, TOM!

TOM. OH MAN!

  (They freak out again.)

  *(**TOM** grabs the laptop. **BRIDGET** grabs **TOM**'s hand. They run out of the hotel room.)*

  (The FBI suite disappears.)

  *(Lights come up on **SYLVIA**'s suite:)*

Sylvia's Hotel Suite at El Tropical

  *(**BRIDGET**, **TOM**, **VERA**, and **DINO** all spill into **SYLVIA**'s suite.)*

BRIDGET. *(To **VERA**.)* Where have you been? You were running the game, weren't you?

VERA. You find out Tom's a secret Fed and *I'm* the one getting yelled at?

DINO. *(To* **TOM.***)* A secret Fed?! I knew it! You ARE an on-duty cop!

TOM. You know, I'm really starting to rethink my line of work.

> *(***SYLVIA*** enters from the bedroom. She's wearing a bathrobe and her presence goes unnoticed as everyone continues to bicker.)*

BRIDGET. *(To* **VERA.***)* If you hadn't been so selfish, none of this would have happened!

VERA. I don't like your tone young lady!

TOM. Confrontation makes me really anxious and I think we should all stop yelling.

VERA & DINO. Shut up!

BRIDGET. Hey! You can't yell at him! Only I can yell at him!

> *(Everyone but* **TOM** *starts yelling again.)*

SYLVIA. ENOUGH!

TOM. GIA'S COMING AND WE ARE ALL GONNA DIE!!!!!!

> *(He hugs* **SYLVIA***'s legs.)*

I have evidence recorded on my laptop.

> *(***SYLVIA** *pats his head.)*

SYLVIA. That's good. We can use that!
(To everyone else.) You're all scared. And that's OK. I'm scared too. But we are a FAMILY. And you know what family does when things get tough?

DINO. Yell at each other?

> *(They all look at* **DINO.***)*

What? I'm Italian. If we're not yelling, we're dead.

SYLVIA. OK, sure. Families yell, and they fight, but it all comes from a place of love. And when things get tough, a family works together to survive.

VERA. Yeah!

SYLVIA. And a family does what they have to!

BRIDGET. Yeah!

SYLVIA. And THIS family is going to do exactly what I tell them to, without any arguments.

DINO. But –

SYLVIA. NO ARGUMENTS. Nana's got a plan. Tom, is that computer of yours fully charged?

TOM. Sure is.

SYLVIA. And can you show my how to make a sound recording?

TOM. Yeah!

SYLVIA. And I'm assuming you have a partner?

TOM. Pssh. Boy do I. Wait till you meet 'em.

VERA. They're very strange.

SYLVIA. Good. We'll need to get in touch with them. Now let's go!

> *(Everyone heads toward the door of the suite.)*

> *(**SYLVIA** stops them.)*

Not that way! This way.

> *(She points to her bedroom.)*

We're all gonna change for my show.

BRIDGET. Nana, our lives are in danger and you want us to go watch your floor show?

SYLVIA. There's no place safer in this whole casino than in front of an audience, Bridget.

> *(**SYLVIA** exits into the bedroom area of the suite.)*

> *(**DINO**, **TOM**, **VERA**, and **BRIDGET** all follow after her.)*

> *(Lights out.)*

> *(Music up. Something vintage*.)*

---

* A license to produce *Nana Does Vegas* does not include a performance license for any third-party or copyrighted recordings. Licensees should create their own.

Scene Two

Optional Scene: The Silver Belles Floor Show

(Ideally, while the main cast is executing the quick change, you'd have three to six **SHOWGIRLS**, *dressed in costumes similar to the ones on* **SYLVIA**'s *mannequins, come out on stage and start doing a number from the floor show.)*

(They'll dance and dance, shimmy and shake...and at the end of the number, a very awkward looking group of three more **SHOWGIRLS** *will join them [exactly dressed as* **SYLVIA**'s *mannequins because, well, it's those costumes], and try to keep up with the dancing [this is* **DINO**, **TOM**, *and* **VERA**, *all undercover].)*

*(***TOM** *and* **DINO** *will keep their faces hidden by their fans the whole time, which will hopefully make their dancing even more awkward and hilarious.)*

*(***VERA** *is having a blast. And she's kind of great at dancing.)*

(Once the number is done [or if you can't do this scene], the **SHOWGIRLS** *will dance off stage and we'll wheel out...)*

Scene Three

El Tropical High-stakes Roulette Table

(Sound cues: Applause! Music*! It's the end of **SYLVIA***'s show.)*

(A few high rollers sit at the table. **GIA** *included, but she has her eye on the "door" to the theater.)*

(Which is too bad for her, because if she paid attention, she would notice that **BRIDGET** *and* **SYLVIA** *[in disguise] are at the high-stakes roulette table, gambling [and watching* **GIA***, anxiously].)*

ANNOUNCER'S VOICE. Let's hear it one more time for the Belles of the Tropic! And don't forget, you can join our showgirls out on the casino floor, tell 'em what a swell time you had!

*(***FRANK*** enters from the "door" to the theater. Sees* **GIA***.)*

FRANK. Boy! That was a swell show. You see it?

*(***GIA*** glares at him.)*

GIA. No.

FRANK. I'm gonna get some of them dancing girls' autographs! You really missed out, lady!

GIA. I'll catch it next time.

(Vera's **BELLBOY** *enters.)*

*(***GIA*** grabs him and pulls him aside.)*

Well? Did you find the costume designer and her entourage?

---

* A license to produce *Nana Does Vegas* does not include a performance license for any third-party or copyrighted recordings. Licensees should create their own.

(A **SHOWGIRL** *enters from the theater area.)*

(If you're paying close attention, you'll notice that this outfit looks an awful lot like one of the ones from **SYLVIA**'s *dress mannequin.)*

BELLBOY. Just saw them!

GIA. Spit. It. Out.

BELLBOY. They went back up to her suite.

GIA. You're sure?

BELLBOY. Yeah. They seemed real nervous, too.

*(***GIA*** smiles. Pats his head.)*

(He holds out his hand for a tip.)

*(***GIA*** slaps his hand.)*

GIA. Thank you. I just need to go up to my room and grab my violin case.

BELLBOY. What are you going to do? Play them a tune?

GIA. Yeah. A SWAN SONG.

(She laughs psychotically and exits.)

(Another **SHOWGIRL** *enters. A fan covers their face... They follow* **GIA** *offstage. At a distance.)*

(A third **SHOWGIRL** *enters. A fan covers their face, too.)*

(The two remaining **SHOWGIRLS** *begin schmoozing with the high as the lights dim on them.)*

El Tropical High-Stakes Roulette Table and Sylvia's Suite

*(***VERA**, **DINO*** and **TOM** *stand together in* **SYLVIA**'s *suite. Or, at least, it kinda looks like they're standing there. But guys. They aren't!*

It's just **SYLVIA***'s dress mannequins wearing* **VERA, DINO,** *and* **TOM***'s clothes!)*

VERA'S VOICE. What do we do now?

DINO'S VOICE. Just keep quiet.

(Beep! The sound of a keycard in the lock.)

(The door to **SYLVIA***'s suite inches open.)*

BRIDGET'S VOICE. Can we turn the lights on at least?

SYLVIA'S VOICE. No!

TOM'S VOICE. This is a horrible idea. We shouldn't have come back here.

DINO'S VOICE. Hey! You second guessing me?

*(***GIA** *steps into the room. Maybe with another* **THUG** *if you have an extra human to spare.)*

GIA. SURPRISE!

(They open fire in the room. Bam-bam-bam-bam-bam-bam.)

(If you can, maybe the mannequins explode confetti or something!)

And that's how it's done.

VERA'S VOICE. What do we do now?

DINO'S VOICE. Just keep quiet!

GIA. Hey, wait a minute!

*(***GIA** *switches on the lights.)*

(Reveal: the mannequins. And **TOM***'s computer, open on the dining room table, playing a recording of their voices.)*

Those aren't people! They're dummies!

*(***JO** *and* **TOM** *[wearing a showgirl outfit] bust into the suite, handcuff* **GIA** *and her* **THUG***.)*

JO. Gia Mastropietro, you are under arrest!

GIA. You gotta be kidding me!

TOM. *(Dead serious and seemingly unaware of his ridiculous outfit.)* This is no joke.

(As they march **GIA** *out of the room –)*

JO. *(To* **TOM**.*)* You know, you kinda pull that outfit off.

(At the roulette table, the other two showgirls reveal their faces: it's **VERA***! And* **DINO***!)*

*(***BRIDGET*** *and* **SYLVIA** *rip off their disguises too!)*

(The **BELLBOY** *comes up to* **VERA** *and they high five.)*

VERA. Good work, kid!

*(***VERA*** *hands him a wad of cash.)*

BELLBOY. Anything for you, Vera.

(He leaves.)

*(***BRIDGET*** *is still anxious –* **SYLVIA** *puts an arm around her.)*

SYLVIA. Don't worry! I'm sure it went fine –

*(***TOM***,* **JO***,* **GIA** *[and her* **THUG***] enter.* **GIA** *mid-perp walk.)*

DINO. There they are!

TOM. *(Excitedly.)* Bridget! Look! My first perp walk!

DINO. That boy is so strange.

BRIDGET. *(To* **DINO**.*)* I know. Isn't it the best?

JO. *(To* **TOM**.*)* Go ahead. I can take it from here.

*(***JO*** *and* **GIA** *exit.)*

*(***TOM*** *rushes over to join* **BRIDGET***,* **DINO***,* **VERA***, and* **SYLVIA**.*)*

TOM. Man, Gia started confessing as soon as we got in the elevator! She's gonna flip on her whole family!

*(***SYLVIA*** *glances over at* **DINO**.*)*

SYLVIA. Is that bad news for you?

DINO. Me? Nah. Worst I ever done crime-wise is fudge my taxes.

(He shrugs.)

I may look very intimidating –

(A beat as they all take in his showgirl appearance...about as far away from intimidating as you can get.)

But I'm really just a teddy bear.

(SYLVIA hugs him.)

SYLVIA. You're MY teddy bear.

DINO. Hey, Vera – with Gia's testimony, El Tropical will finally be out from under the Mastropietro family. So what do you say? You wanna manage this casino with me?

VERA. Only if I get to be a dealer at the domino tables whenever I want.

(She grins.)

I got some Whales who would miss their favorite sailor.

DINO. It's a deal!

(They shake.)

VERA. I'm gonna go scope out where my dominoes tables will go! We should get rid of some of those slot machines –

(She walks off.)

(DINO follows after her –)

DINO. Now, hang on – the slot machines are a huge money maker!

(DINO and VERA exit.)

BRIDGET. You really saved the day, Nana.

TOM. Thank you, Sylvia.

SYLVIA. Anything for my two favorite grandchildren. Now, excuse me. I think I have to go referee a fight between Vera and Dino.

BRIDGET. Your work is never done, is it? This family is so lucky to have you, Nana.

(**SYLVIA** *beams.*)

SYLVIA. I'm the lucky one.

(*As she exits –*)

Vera! Knock it off!

TOM. (*To* **BRIDGET**.) So...are we still getting married? After all the lies and the yelling and...well – this outfit?

(**BRIDGET** *laughs, puts her arms around* **TOM**.)

BRIDGET. (*Playfully.*) I will marry you on two conditions.

TOM. Oh yeah? And they are?

BRIDGET. No more lies.

TOM. Done. What's the second condition?

BRIDGET. You gotta do that little dance you did on stage again for me.

TOM. What? This dance?

(*He does a little dance move.*)

(**BRIDGET** *laughs and claps.*)

BRIDGET. That's the one.

(*He grabs* **BRIDGET** *and they do a little dance move together. He dips her and kisses her.*)

TOM. You can't tell any of the guys on the force about this.

BRIDGET. I won't. Because you know what they say about Vegas, Tom.

TOM. ...It's a desert climate so drink lots of water?

(**BRIDGET** *laughs.*)

BRIDGET. Something like that.

(*They kiss again.*)

(*Music. Maybe a song about Vegas. For obvious reasons*.)

---

* A license to produce *Nana Does Vegas* does not include a performance license for any third-party or copyrighted recordings. Licensees should create their own.

(The rest of the cast dances out on stage.)

(They take their bows. And –)

End of Play

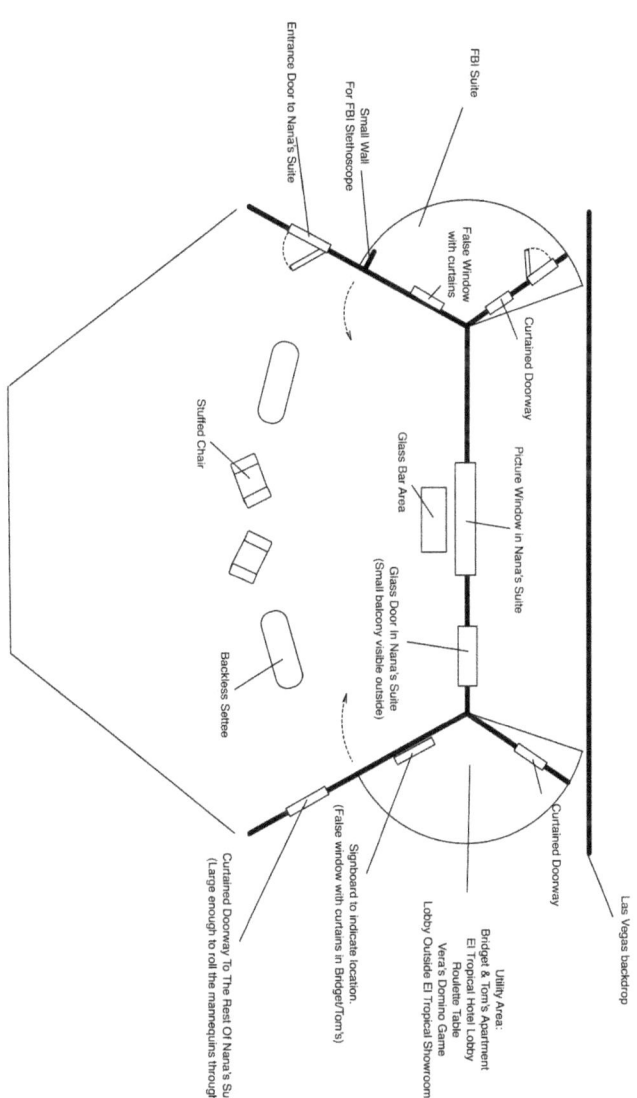

Entrance Door to Nana's Suite

Small Wall
For FBI Stethoscope

FBI Suite

False Window
with curtains

Curtained Doorway

Stuffed Chair

Glass Bar Area

Picture Window in Nana's Suite

Glass Door In Nana's Suite
(Small balcony visible outside)

Backless Settee

Curtained Doorway

Las Vegas backdrop

Curtained Doorway To The Rest Of Nana's Suite
(Large enough to roll the mannequins through)

Signboard to indicate location.
(False window with curtains in Bridget/Tom's)

Utility Area:
Bridget & Tom's Apartment
El Tropical Hotel Lobby
Roulette Table
Vera's Domino Game
Lobby Outside El Tropical Showroom

Set design by Cynthia Haynes DiSavino